KICK

ALSO BY WALTER DEAN MYERS

FICTION

Autobiography of My Dead Brother
NATIONAL BOOK AWARD FINALIST

Crystal

Dope Sick
ALA TOP TEN QUICK PICK FOR
RELUCTANT YOUNG ADULT READERS

The Dream Bearer
NEW YORK PUBLIC LIBRARY BOOK FOR THE TEEN AGE

Game

Handbook for Boys: A Novel

It Ain't All for Nothin'

Lockdown
NATIONAL BOOK AWARD FINALIST

Looking for the Easy Life

Monster
MICHAEL L. PRINTZ AWARD
CORETTA SCOTT KING AUTHOR HONOR BOOK
NATIONAL BOOK AWARD FINALIST

The Mouse Rap

Patrol: An American Soldier in Vietnam
JANE ADDAMS CHILDREN'S BOOK AWARD

The Righteous Revenge of Artemis Bonner

Scorpions
NEWBERY HONOR BOOK

Shooter
CHILDREN'S BOOK SENSE SUMMER PICK

The Story of the Three Kingdoms

Street Love
KIRKUS BEST CHILDREN'S BOOK OF THE YEAR

NONFICTION

Bad Boy: A Memoir
PARENTS' CHOICE GOLD AWARD

Brown Angels: An Album of Pictures and Verse

Ida B. Wells: Let the Truth Be Told

I've Seen the Promised Land:
The Life of Dr. Martin Luther King, Jr.

Malcolm X: A Fire Burning Brightly

Muhammad Ali: The People's Champion

Now Is Your Time!:
The African-American Struggle for Freedom
CORETTA SCOTT KING AUTHOR AWARD

WALTER DEAN MYERS
AND ROSS WORKMAN

KICK

HARPER TEEN

An Imprint of HarperCollinsPublishers

HarperTeen is an imprint of HarperCollins Publishers.

Kick
www.harperteen.com

Library of Congress Cataloging-in-Publication Data
Myers, Walter Dean, date
   Kick / Walter Dean Myers and Ross Workman. — 1st ed.
      p. cm.
   Summary: Told in their separate voices, thirteen-year-old
soccer star Kevin and police sergeant Brown, his mentor, try
to keep Kevin out of juvenile hall after he is arrested on very
serious charges.
   ISBN 978-0-06-200489-5 (trade bdg.)
   ISBN 978-0-06-200490-1 (lib. bdg.)
   [1. Conduct of life—Fiction. 2. Criminal investigation—
Fiction. 3. Police—Fiction. 4. Soccer—Fiction. 5. Family
problems—Fiction. 6. Mentoring—Fiction. 7. New Jersey—
Fiction. 8. Youths' writings.] I. Workman, Ross. II. Title.
PZ7.M992Kic 2011   2010018441
[Fic]—dc22   CIP
                                                            AC

Typography by Andrea Vandergrift
11 12 13 14 15   LP/RRDB   10 9 8 7 6 5 4 3 2 1
❖
First Edition

Turning and turning in the widening gyre

The falcon cannot hear the falconer;

Things fall apart; the centre cannot hold;

Mere anarchy is loosed upon the world,

The blood-dimmed tide is loosed, and everywhere

The ceremony of innocence is drowned;

The best lack all conviction, while the worst

Are full of passionate intensity.

—William Butler Yeats (1865–1939),

"The Second Coming"

CHAPTER
01

Bill Kelly and I had been friends since we played high school basketball together. I had played strong forward and he had been the quick guard with the sweet outside shot. He had always been bright and the kind of kid who did his homework on time and worried about his grades, and I was always more relaxed. After high school I went into the army and then onto the police force, and Bill went on to law school. I knew he would do well and he did, but he really came into his own when he became a judge. He always seemed to look to do a bit more than he had to, for the community as well as for the people who came through his courtroom. So when he called me and asked me if I would mind coming down to his office to talk about a case he had an interest in, I was flattered.

It was only a twenty-minute drive from my place to the Highland Municipal Courthouse. I parked in the rear of the old Art Deco structure, went through the double doors and past the cafeteria, and made my way to the elevator bank in the east end of the building.

Judge Kelly's office was on the third floor, and I arrived at two minutes to the hour.

Miss Weinberg, Kelly's secretary, smiled as she picked up the phone.

"Sergeant Brown is here, sir," she said.

A moment later the frosted door opened and Judge Kelly, nearly as lean as he had been in his playing days, stepped out.

"Come on in, Jerry," he said, extending his hand. "How you doing these days?"

"I'm good," I said. "Fighting the battle of the bulge. Looks like even the salads are fattening these days."

"You need to come jogging with me," he said, going behind his desk.

I noticed that there was a young officer already seated in one of the chairs facing the judge.

"Sergeant Jerry Brown, this is Scott Evans. He made the arrest of the young man I'm interested in," Judge Kelly said.

"Hey, how's it going?" The young officer stood and extended his hand.

"It's going well," I answered.

"Sergeant Brown's been interested in keeping young people out of trouble for a long time, and as I mentioned to you before, we've talked about cases in which we might be able to intervene and keep a kid on the right path," Judge Kelly said. "This young man's father was a policeman."

"Was?" I asked.

"You remember Johnson? Young officer who got caught up in a shoot-out a few years ago?" Kelly leaned back in his chair and clasped his hands behind his neck.

"Yeah. He was a good young . . . his kid is in trouble?" I looked at the arresting officer.

"Scott, why don't you fill Jerry in?" Judge Kelly asked the officer.

Evans took out his pad, took a few seconds to read his notes, then looked up at me.

"I was on patrol last night, just after nine, when I saw a Ford Taurus driving erratically along the street parallel to the highway. The lights weren't on and the car was weaving. I thought it was a drunk and I put my lights on. When I did that, the car sped up a bit, then braked, then sped up and skidded into a light pole. No major damages, but I got the feeling whoever was driving was just lucky at that time. I told them over the loudspeaker to turn the engine off, and they complied. Then I ordered them out of the car.

"At first I thought it was an old skinny guy and then I saw that it was a kid. I checked the car and there was a passenger, and she looked even younger than the driver. Okay, so I figured a couple of kids making out in a moving car. I asked the kid for his driver's license and he doesn't have one. I asked him how old he was, and he looks at me and says he's thirteen. I put my light on his face and I see he's *really* young. His name is Kevin Johnson."

"His parents' car?" I asked.

"No, it's the girl's father's car," Evans said. "She's thirteen, and I look at her face and I see she's been crying. Her face is all puffy and red. I take the guy to the back of the car and ask him what's going on. He gives me a 'Nothing.' So I cuff him and tell him to sit on the sidewalk next to the car, and I go to the girl and I ask her what's going on. She gives me the same 'Nothing.' Which, incidentally, pisses me off. I don't know the kid is the son of a policeman who was killed in the line of duty."

"You couldn't know that," Judge Kelly said.

"So I get the girl's ID and her telephone number and I call her house. I get the father and tell him I just stopped two kids in his car and ask him if he knows anything about it."

"What did he say?" I asked.

"At first he doesn't say anything, and then, after he's been thinking for a minute, he says the kid driving must have stolen it and made the girl go along. Okay, so it's a stolen car rap, kidnapping, driving without a license, damaging city property—the light pole—plus traffic violations. McNamara, that's the girl's father, says he doesn't have another car and he's going to have to walk to where we were. I tell him to stay home and

I'll bring the girl to his house."

"Which is where?" I asked.

"Elystan Place," Evans said. "Over past the water tower."

"Okay."

"So I take the girl home and I ask the father if he wants to press charges, because the charges can be pretty steep," Evans continued. "Meanwhile I'm checking out the girl and she's looking down and the father's looking away from her, and the boy, Kevin, is just sitting in my car with his head down."

"Something's going on," I said.

"Yeah, but nobody's talking, so I asked the father again does he want to press charges, and he says yes," Scott says. "Then I asked the girl if the boy did anything to her. If he hit her or touched her in any way, and she says no.

"The father tells me that his wife is sick and is it okay if he comes down to the station to press charges in the morning, and I said it was and told him where to come. That's it."

"You asked the girl if the boy hit her or touched her," I said. "What did the father say? Did he look upset?"

Scott hesitated, then shook his head. "No, he just took the girl into the house."

"According to the precinct desk sergeant, the father came in this morning and asked a lot of questions about what would happen if he pressed charges and what would happen if he didn't," Judge Kelly said. "He wanted to know if the girl would have to testify."

"What was your take on the situation?" I asked Officer Evans. "Did you think this boy—what's his name?"

"Kevin, Kevin Johnson."

"You get the impression Kevin was forcing the girl into anything?"

"I wasn't sure," Evans said, leaning forward in his chair. "But as she turned to walk into the house, she looked back at him and smiled. I didn't know if it meant anything, but she smiled like she was saying everything was okay between them."

"And how did he look?"

"His eyes were working," Evans said. "He was looking around and thinking hard, but he kept his mouth shut. I asked him on the way to the station if he thought he was a tough guy."

"What did he say?"

"Nothing. Not a word."

"So what do you want me to do?" I asked Judge Kelly.

"Jerry, when we were talking about the program

at the club, I knew we were thinking about young African-American kids," Judge Kelly said, pushing a file folder across the desk. "This kid isn't African American, but he is a police officer's son, and maybe a good young man. He's got no record. No trouble at school. I think McNamara, the girl's father, might not press charges. I don't know. This whole case is up in the air right now and can land in a lot of places. If you have the time to look into it . . . "

"I'll see what I can do," I said, standing.

I thanked Evans and took the file.

On the way home I thought again about the meeting at the club and talk about mentoring teenagers. A priest who was there, somewhat less enthusiastic than the rest of us, had talked about how complex some of the situations could get.

I stopped at Holes!, the donut shop on Evergreen, and bought a dozen donuts—six glazed and six unglazed—and a medium coffee. The parking area was almost empty, and I thumbed through the file as I drank the coffee. There was no picture of young Mr. Johnson and I wondered what he looked like. I imagined a surly kid with a slightly turned-up lip and a squint.

I hadn't known his father personally, but I remembered

the funeral of the young Irish-American officer and knew I must have seen the family. Every police funeral is a tragedy as far as I am concerned, and I never wanted to dwell on them.

The girl, Christy, and her family lived in the Brunswick section of town, a neighborhood that had changed a lot since I was a kid. It had been an industrial area, had declined for a while, but now was recovering as the old buildings were being converted into condos to attract an upscale crowd. I recalled there had been an investigation of possible exploitation of immigrant workers in the area.

I drove home, transferred half the donuts to another plastic bag, and put them in the glove compartment. Carolyn would never understand the pressures that demanded a full dozen. Inside the house, I called Gracie at the precinct and asked her to run a search on Michael McNamara, the girl's father.

"Drunk and disorderly, two years ago. He slapped his wife around a bit but she refused to get an order of protection. And a citation four years ago for illegal parking. You in the office baseball pool this week?"

"I never win the darn thing."

"Stop whining, Jerry—you in it or not?"

"I'm in it," I said.

Carolyn saw the bag of donuts on the coffee table and gave me the Look. "Have you forgotten everything the doctor told you?" she asked.

I put on my best wounded face and handed over the sinful six.

CHAPTER
02

I kept my head down as I watched shoes pass me by. Shiny black high heels clicking against the floor. Beat-up white Nikes spotted with dirt stains. I sat shivering in the waiting room of the Bedford County Juvenile Detention Center. They had turned the air conditioner up extra high. I bet it was to make us feel even worse than we did just being in this place. My head was spinning and I felt sick to my stomach. I couldn't believe I was locked up. I kept asking myself why I was in this place. I was no criminal.

But I knew I couldn't tell the truth.

My wrists burned from the handcuffs that the police had put on me when I was arrested. My shoulders ached. The cot they had assigned me felt like concrete. Not that I could sleep anyway. The whole night was playing over and over in my head, like a bad movie I couldn't forget. I just wanted this mess to be over and to go home.

But I didn't know how I would face Mom. The worst part about everything last night was seeing Mom when she came to the precinct. It wasn't like she was mad, just horribly disappointed and sad.

In the middle of the night I woke up to find the door being swung open. An officer was uncuffing another inmate. The kid was older than me.

"Happy to be back home, Morales?" the officer said.

"I know you missed me," the kid shot back.

"Yeah, but I figured I'd see you again."

I tried not to look at the kid as he got settled in.

The tattoos on his shoulders ran down his arms. I wondered if he was in a gang, but I definitely wasn't going to ask him. I pretended to be asleep.

In the morning they brought us out to breakfast, and there were two fights before we reached the food counter. Some of the guys looked too old to be in a juvenile detention center. I wondered if some of them were in gangs, because they were flashing signs at each other. I liked to watch a show on TV called *Gangland,* where real gang members came and talked about the history of their gangs and what they did as members. But this wasn't TV. This was my life. I wished it wasn't.

The food was greasy. I wouldn't have eaten it even if my stomach felt okay.

After breakfast the guards walked us back to our cells. The uniforms we had to wear were a dull gray, which matched our moods.

The guy in my cell, Morales, asked if I had been arraigned yet. I shook my head no. I didn't know what he was talking about, but I didn't want to ask him.

"That's when you find out what's gonna happen to you," he said. "Don't be acting too tough, man. Maybe you can cop a break."

The guy looked hard, and every other word that came out of his mouth was a curse.

He told me what was wrong with the place and who to avoid. I was surprised he was friendly. But he also seemed mad at the world, like it had given up on him.

The whole time he was talking, I could feel my heart

beating against the inside of my chest. It didn't feel like a tough heartbeat, either.

All morning I sat around trying to think through what was happening, but I was too scared to concentrate. When the guard came and called my name, I hardly recognized it. He said I had a visitor in the interview room. I hoped it was Mom. I hoped it was her even though I felt terrible about her seeing me in jail.

The interview room was painted a pale white. I glanced up at the clock every now and then; it was behind a metal grille, like it was locked up, too. I imagined all the things a clock would have done to be in here. I guess he'd have to do his time, I thought. I laughed for the first time since the arrest.

I sat alone on the hard plastic chair for nearly fifteen minutes before the door opened. I watched a pair of big brown shoes stop just inside the door and then step toward me. I slowly lifted my head. A tall black man with broad shoulders, wearing a shirt and tie, looked down at me with surprise on his face.

"Kevin Johnson?" he asked.

"Yes," I said, standing. I wondered what he wanted with me.

"I'm Sergeant Jerry Brown," he said, putting out

his hand. I shook it. "Hear you got yourself into some trouble, huh?"

I nodded.

"You want to tell me about it?"

"Not really." He couldn't expect me to tell him anything. I didn't even know him.

He sat down in the chair next to me. I hoped he was as uncomfortable as I was in the hard plastic seat.

"Kevin, let me tell you something about myself. I'm a police officer just like the one who arrested you. Just like your father was. Judge Kelly asked me to look into your case because he had a lot of respect for your father. I did, too," he said. "I'd like to try to help you if I can. You know the charges, don't you?"

"Driving without a license," I said.

"Driving without a . . . ?" He looked away and then back at me. "Try kidnapping, grand theft auto, destruction of property, and giving false answers. We're talking felonies, not misdemeanors."

Kidnapping? I didn't know they charged me for kidnapping! They got it all wrong.

I tried to stay calm. "A felony? What's that?"

"It's a really serious type of crime, Kevin."

"I didn't do anything."

15

"Weren't you driving a car that crashed last night? You could do yourself a favor and tell me now, or if you want, you can do it in front of twelve other people who couldn't care less about you."

"So, why do *you* care what happens to me?"

Sergeant Brown raised his eyebrows. "Judge Kelly said you needed some straightening out. He asked me if I wanted to help you and I said I'd give it a try. But you need to be honest with me. With some straight answers and a little luck, you might, just might, not have to stay in here. You *are* interested in getting out?"

Sergeant Brown spoke in a voice that meant business. He looked at me, waiting for my answer.

"All I want to do is go home," I said.

"It's not that simple, young man," Sergeant Brown said. "You're going to have to go to the judge's chambers and explain a lot of things to him. And tell them in a way to make him think you deserve to leave here tonight."

"I'm not that good at explaining things," I said. "The cop who handcuffed me didn't believe me."

Sergeant Brown kind of puffed up, shook his head a little, and exhaled. "Just what *are* you good at?" he asked.

16

"I don't know. Soccer, I guess," I answered. "But that's not going to help me in here, is it? The tournament lottery is tomorrow."

"Which means . . . ?"

"The lottery for the State Cup. That's the most important soccer tournament in New Jersey. The brackets will be posted tomorrow, so we'll know what team we're playing first round."

"You're in jail for a bunch of felonies and you're thinking about soccer?"

"I don't know what to think about," I said. "I don't even know if I'm thinking straight."

That shut him up for a few minutes.

"So, Kevin, what position do you play?" Sergeant Brown asked me.

"Striker," I said.

"Is that defense or offense?" Sergeant Brown asked.

"You don't know anything about soccer, right?" I asked.

"Not really," he answered. "And you don't know much about the law, so maybe we can both learn something. What do you think?"

"Sounds okay, I guess."

Sergeant Brown stood up. "Now we're going to talk it over with your mom," he said. "Then we're going to meet with Judge Kelly and see if he wants to keep you in here."

"Keep me in here!" Maybe I should have been a little nicer to this man. I wanted to throw up.

The door to the room inched open, and my mom and grandma slowly came in. Mom's face was stained with tears. Abuela, my grandma, seemed smaller as she walked behind Mom. They took seats across from Sergeant Brown and me.

About four years ago my *abuelo* died. That's when Abuela came from Colombia to live with us. I loved her almost as much as I loved Mom. Mom worked six days a week as an assistant in a doctor's office. Abuela had been taking care of me since I was nine.

"Ay, mi nieto." Abuela sounded so sad. She put her hands on my cheeks.

I could see that tears were welling up in the corners of her eyes. I felt like crying, too, but I didn't want to cry in front of Sergeant Brown.

"Mom, this is Sergeant Brown," I said softly. "He wants to talk to you."

18

"Nice to meet you," my mom said politely, her voice cracking.

I hated to see my mom sad. She'd already been through so much.

"Abuela, le presento al señor Brown," I said, introducing Abuela to Sergeant Brown in Spanish.

Sergeant Brown turned to my mom. "Ma'am, I'm a police officer and also a friend of Judge Kelly. He asked me if I would look into Kevin's case. We'll be talking to the judge in a few minutes, and I'm hoping that everything will turn out all right, but there are a lot of unknown aspects to this case. Most important is that Kevin needs to explain what happened."

"Kevin's a good boy," Mom said. "He really is. Believe me, he's never been in any kind of serious trouble."

"I believe you, and I'm sure you want him home. If he gets to go home, I'll be talking with him from time to time as the case develops. Is that okay with you? Now I'm going to be frank with you. Your son's in trouble. He's up against serious charges. I'm sure that if Kevin gets out and there's the least bit of trouble, he's coming back here."

"I really appreciate your taking an interest in my son,

sir." My mom sat back in her chair, her hands shaking with nervousness.

"Well, we don't want our young people in jails if we can help it, ma'am," Sergeant Brown said.

Sergeant Brown kept talking to Mom and Abuela. I thought about this television show where two cops were interviewing a guy. One was playing the "good cop" role and the other one was the "bad cop." I wondered if Sergeant Brown was playing good cop or bad cop.

Mom kept nodding to anything Sergeant Brown said. Abuela just looked at me and kept shaking her head. I was glad when a guard came into the room. Judge Kelly was ready to see us.

The guards drove me in a van to the Highland Municipal Courthouse. It was an old brick building with white columns in the front that looked like something on the cover of my social studies textbook. Mrs. Fox, the lawyer who had handled the paperwork when my dad died, was waiting for us in the hallway. I walked in with the guard behind me. I was relieved to see a familiar face, even though I really didn't know her that well.

It was weird having someone watch my every move. I

noticed the guard's gun. When I was little, my dad used to show me his gun. He always warned me about how dangerous guns were, and I used to think it was so cool. But now that the guard who was watching me had one, guns didn't seem so cool anymore. The guard saw me staring at his gun. I turned away.

I didn't even want to imagine what my father would say if he were still alive. I had just been helping out a friend.

After going through the metal detectors, Mom, Abuela, the guard, and I walked down the hall and up a long flight of stairs to the judge's chambers with Sergeant Brown trailing behind.

Judge Kelly was the tallest man I had ever seen. I wondered if he had ever played basketball. His wire-rimmed glasses made him look smart. I imagined him playing college ball. My mom, Abuela, and I took seats, and Mrs. Fox started speaking in low tones to the judge. I could tell that it was about me.

"Mr. Johnson, I presume," Judge Kelly said, his glasses lowering on his nose.

"Yes. Nice to meet you, sir," I answered, standing up and trying to be extra polite.

"Jerry! How are you?" Judge Kelly said.

I turned around to see Sergeant Brown sitting behind us.

"Up for another game of Ping-Pong at the Ebony Club?" asked Sergeant Brown.

"Not tonight—I'm swamped with work," Judge Kelly said, looking right at me.

Judge Kelly turned to me. "So, Kevin, you're charged with kidnapping, grand larceny, destruction of property, and giving false answers."

"Yes, sir," I said.

Mrs. Fox interrupted, "Judge Kelly, Kevin has never been in any sort of trouble before. The only reasonable solution would be to give him probation."

"We're going to give him every break we can under the law," Judge Kelly said. "There are a number of issues to be worked out first. This is not a victimless affair, and the victims' rights have to be considered, too. Frankly, I don't understand how the son of one of our town's finest police officers could have gotten involved in something like this. Kevin, can you explain yourself?"

"I just . . . just did it, I guess," I said. "I'm so sorry." There were things I couldn't really explain.

Judge Kelly frowned at me. He could frown at me

all he wanted, but I still didn't want to get a friend in trouble.

"I'd like some time to look into the matter if the court will allow that." Sergeant Brown spoke up. "Kevin has good family ties, and as his attorney points out, he has a clean record."

"It can't take forever, Jerry," Judge Kelly said. "Our calendars are crammed. I don't have to tell you that."

"No, sir," Sergeant Brown said, crossing one leg over the other.

"I'll either dispose of the case in three weeks or send it to another judge," Judge Kelly said. "In the meantime, I'm going to release young Mr. Johnson to his mother."

As soon as I heard that, I wanted to thank Judge Kelly and Sergeant Brown over and over again.

I had to pick up my clothes and Mom had to sign a bunch of forms at the detention center so I could leave. I couldn't believe I was out so quick.

In the car on the way home, I could feel the tension.

My mom finally broke the silence. "Kevin, if you get yourself into any trouble at all, even if you're just with someone who gets in trouble, you're going to be sent back in there. You have to be careful who you hang around with. Do you understand that?" Mom was so upset, she didn't even turn around to look at me as she was talking. "I can't believe this is happening to our family."

That was about as close as my mom ever got to raising her voice. "I'm so sorry, Mom," I answered. And I meant it. Even though I had only been locked up for one night, I never wanted to go back to that place again.

Abuela always talked too much, but she had nothing to say to me now. That was almost worse.

We made one stop at a bakery to pick up some *almojábanas*—Colombian breads filled with cheese. This was my favorite food. Even though she was mad, Mom was being extra nice, but I wasn't hungry.

On our way home, we drove downtown. It wasn't the weekend, but there were groups of kids from my school hanging around. I closed my eyes and slumped down in my seat. I knew they would have heard about me getting arrested and I'd have to answer a million questions from them.

I thought about Christy. I wondered if she was as scared as I was. I remembered that when the cop had pulled us over, I had turned to her and she hadn't said a word. The cop that had arrested me thought she was just too scared to talk, but I knew there were things that were just too hard to say. Sergeant Brown seemed all right; at least he got me out of juvie. And he didn't feel sorry for me like my mom and grandma did. I liked that.

As we drove along, I saw the green turf of Highland Field shining under the lights. The facility had been built recently after a long, heated argument between the town council members and the taxpayers. My mom used to joke that I'd better enjoy the new soccer fields because the money for them came straight out of her pocket.

Now I wondered whether I'd ever get to play soccer again.

CHAPTER
03

The Johnson boy's family seemed like good people. They did what I had seen a lot of families do, look closely at the person in trouble to see if there was suddenly something different about them, something they hadn't seen before. The mother was holding her hands to her chest while the grandmother, a small woman who carried herself with her head high, kept touching the boy. I got the feeling they both would have liked to take a break and just hold him for a while.

I wanted to know what and who I was dealing with and how serious the case was going to be. If McNamara was definitely going to press charges, then the criminal aspect of the case was going to be the most important.

His home number was listed on the complaint sheet and I called it, introduced myself, and asked if he would be free to talk sometime the next day.

He worked at Harmon Brothers Delivery Service and suggested a place we could meet for lunch.

"I only get an hour," he said.

"Hey, that's fine," I answered. "Meet you there at twelve thirty."

The Celebrity Diner was one of those old-fashioned red-leather-and-chrome places that seemed inviting even on the dreariest days. I got there at twelve twenty, sat in a booth, and ordered coffee. At exactly twelve thirty a thin, angular man came in and looked around. He looked to be about five ten, maybe a hundred and seventy pounds. When he checked his watch, I figured it was McNamara and went over to him.

"Sergeant Brown," I said, offering my hand.

"Oh, I thought you might be in uniform," he said.

The handshake was tentative, almost timid.

We sat in the booth and I asked him how the corned beef was at the Celebrity.

"It's okay," he said, nodding as he spoke. "Most of the sandwiches here are okay."

I looked at the menu again, and when the waitress came over, I ordered the corned beef, a side of fries, and tea. McNamara ordered ham on rye and black coffee.

"So, you think the Giants are going to get it together this year?" I asked.

"Giants?" He looked toward the open window and then back at me.

"The football Giants," I added.

"Oh, yeah, I guess," he said. "They're okay. I think they're okay."

"You work near here?"

"About ten minutes away," he said. "Delivery company. We do pickups and deliveries throughout the year for the stores at three malls in the area. But the real money comes at Christmas, when we handle the overflow for the really big guys. Sometimes I'm sending out trucks so fast, I can hardly keep up with them."

"This whole area is turning into a shopping hub," I said. "That's a good sign."

"Yeah, yeah, it's changing big-time. I used to drive—now I just do dispatch. When I drove, I had to go all the way into New York to pick up cargo," McNamara said. "Today guys can get a full load in Jersey. It's better that way."

"If the money's right," I said.

"Well, the money's better when you're on the road, but it's hard being away from home all the time." He paused as the waitress brought the tea and coffee. "You gotta balance it out. I didn't mind driving, but . . ."

"I never could handle one of those big rigs," I said.

"You gotta have training," McNamara said. "You don't want to be learning to drive no twenty-four footer at seventy miles per hour."

The waitress brought the sandwiches and two little paper cups of what looked like coleslaw.

"I just wanted to get your take on what happened the other night," I said. "You want some fries?"

"No. I've got a nervous stomach," he said.

"*You've* got a nervous stomach?" I held up a French fry. "If my wife caught me eating these, she'd have a fit."

Half smile. Half a head shake.

"The officer at the scene was surprised to find a kid at the wheel," I said.

"Yeah. Well. I knew the car was gone," McNamara said, "I mean, I looked out the window and saw it was gone. You know, I thought for a minute maybe I had parked it around the corner. Sometimes a guy across the street has his pickup in front of my house. He leaves his car in his driveway, and when he's only going to pop in and out—"

"He leaves his car in front of your place?"

"Yeah. No big deal. But then I remembered that it had been in the driveway, so . . . "

"So you called the police?"

"No, not right away. My wife was kind of . . . kind of under the weather. If . . . You want to find out if I'm going to press charges?" he asked.

"Just trying to get your reaction to what happened that night," I said.

"If it goes to trial, will Christy have to testify?"

"It's possible," I said. "We can usually work things out for kids so it's not too hard on them."

"You know, you can't just take the car into a shop these days." McNamara was pushing his sandwich around his plate with his forefinger. "You walk into any shop in this area and you have a dent the size of a . . .

the size of a coffee cup . . . and they want to charge you an arm and a leg."

"You can say that again," I said. "My car was losing its charge too fast, and I took it in and had to shell out six hundred bucks."

"Alternator!"

"The report said the boy was driving was only thirteen," I said, looking for a reaction.

"What did he think?" McNamara was suddenly agitated. "That he could just hop into somebody's car and go joyriding?"

"Was that what he was doing?" I asked.

"I don't know," he said, half under his breath.

"He goes to the same school as your daughter does?"

"Yeah, I seen him around," McNamara said. "Comes to the house sometimes. I think he speaks Spanish to Dolores."

"That your wife?"

"Dolores? No. She kind of helps out around the house sometimes. Christy knows this guy, but *I'm* the only one who can give him permission to drive my car. And I didn't give him permission. He could have been in a serious freaking accident. Sometimes big rigs take the service road if they want to cut off some time. They're not supposed to, but you do what you got to do to make it in this world."

"That's for sure," I said. "Hey, did you know Kevin's father was a cop? Killed in the line of duty."

"What's that supposed to mean? That supposed to mean I'm not supposed to press charges?"

"I didn't say that," I answered. "I was just surprised that a cop's kid would be in this kind of trouble."

"I guess the cops will be looking at me, seeing who I am so they can spring this kid," McNamara said.

"Think you have it wrong," I said. "Nobody's trying to influence you in any way. At least I'm not."

"So what's going to happen next?"

"An assistant district attorney will probably call you and maybe get a statement," I said. "Then there'll be a meeting to see what the charges will be and how the state will handle them."

"Will Christy have to testify?" he asked. Second time.

"She won't have to do anything she doesn't want to do," I said.

"You know, I treat everybody the same," McNamara said. "Half my drivers are either black or Latino. I could be having lunch with any of them the same as I'm having lunch with you. It doesn't matter to me."

"And the sandwiches here are good," I said.

I paid for the lunch and shook McNamara's hand. He had his uneaten sandwich wrapped and took it with him. I didn't see him go to a car in the parking lot. I wondered just how badly his car had been damaged.

My next stop was at Kevin's school. It was an easy drive, and I parked across the street from the ugly, red-brick building next to a playing field teeming with young bodies in a hurry. I sat in the car trying to figure out exactly who McNamara was. On the one hand, he seemed more nervous than I thought he should be, but on the other hand, he was also concerned about the money he thought he might have to put into car repairs. It was possible that he would push the charges just to make sure that they were on record for the insurance company.

It was clear to me, too, that he didn't want to have his daughter testify. I could see that. Testifying at a trial isn't that big a deal, but some people get really uptight about it. I didn't think McNamara was hiding

anything, but he was jumpy. I remembered him saying that Kevin had spoken Spanish to the woman who
helped around the house at times. I didn't care for
the way McNamara had brought it up. People who vol-
unteered how they "treat everybody the same" usually
bothered me.

"You're going to have to move this vehicle, sir." A
voice from next to the car startled me.

"Excuse me?"

"I'm school security." The short man standing next
to my window showed me a small badge. "Cars aren't
allowed to park here. If you don't move the car at once,
I'll call the police."

I reached into my side pocket, took out my wallet, and
opened it so he could see my badge. "I *am* the police,"
I said.

"Oh."

Good response.

I had made an appointment to see the Johnson boy's
principal that afternoon, and after parking the car
where the security man pointed, I followed him up to
her first-floor office.

"Just how serious is this, sir?" Sylvia Grosnickle, the
principal of Highland, settled behind her desk. An

34

intense, balding man she had introduced me to as Kevin's gym teacher and soccer coach was in the office with us.

"We're still looking into it," I said. "Right now, it looks like a thirteen-year-old—maybe two thirteen-year-olds—simply made a few bad decisions. With luck, we can end up giving everybody a lecture and chalking the whole thing up to experience."

"And without luck?" The principal's concern was evident.

"Nobody was actually injured and the damage to the car and the light pole was slight, so it looks good," I said. "Right now we just have the field officer's notes and no official charges. What's Kevin like?"

"Quite bright." Miss Grosnickle picked up a chart from her desk. "He tests very well and performs in the upper fifteen to twenty percent of his class. I think he could do better, but he is thirteen."

"You wouldn't call him a troublemaker, then?"

"Not at all," she answered. "I like him."

I was relieved to hear that. "No problem on the field?" I asked the coach.

"Kevin's okay," he said. "Edgy, but okay."

"Edgy?"

"He's fast enough and he knows the game—you can rely on him to hold his own, usually," Hill said. "But sometimes he'll walk out on the field and his game goes up a notch. You watch him and he's two inches from a yellow card all the time, but he makes things happen."

"Yellow card?"

"When a player makes a minor infraction, he gets a yellow card, a warning," the coach said. "If he makes a major infraction, he gets a red card and he's out of the game. When Kevin loses his temper, he's moving better and he's coming on like he's supposed to."

"You like him?"

"Yeah, I do," Coach Hill said. "I do."

"How about the McNamara girl? How does she do?"

"She's a middle grade student," the principal said. "Very polite."

I thanked the coach and the principal and headed back to my car. Kevin was still a mystery to me. At the juvenile hall he was scared, like he should have been, but every once in a while I could see a flash of anger surface. I believed the principal and the coach when they said they liked him, though. That was a good sign.

I hadn't learned anything really special, just that Kevin hadn't been in any serious trouble in school before, and that he was a pretty good soccer player who reacted to things differently if he lost his temper. I wondered if that night he had somehow lost his temper and done something really stupid.

CHAPTER
04

All morning in school I felt eyes looking at me. Whenever I turned to look at someone who I felt was staring, we'd make eye contact for a brief second before they turned away quickly.

It reminded me of three years ago when my dad died and people looked at me like I was the one who had died. Except this time it was different. I didn't really mind the attention. I didn't think kids would mess around with me.

"Everybody's talking about it," my friend Shawn said before taking a last bite out of his sandwich. We were sitting in the cafeteria at lunchtime.

"Everyone has been looking at me weird in the hallways, like I'm an alien or something," I said.

"Well, not many kids get sent to jail around here." One of his dreadlocks fell over his eye. He was opening a bag of potato chips. "So what happened?"

"I don't want to talk about it." I felt bad not telling Shawn. We'd been friends ever since we were five years old and on the same peewee soccer team at the YMCA.

I put my pizza down. Since I'd been arrested, I'd lost my appetite.

"You going to get to play with us in the State Cup?" Shawn asked.

"I don't know. I haven't seen Coach Hill yet, but he's gonna be really mad. He's always talking about how soccer is all about character, and he's not going to like my character right now."

I changed the subject. "You liking our chances this season, Shawn?"

"I do, but we need to work as a team more. I mean, the other day during practice, Ricky was just dribbling through kids, doing all this fancy footwork and laughing. But when it gets to November, that's not going to work against any good teams and nobody is gonna be laughing. Everyone is just trying to make themselves look good, but our team isn't. You know what I'm saying?"

I nodded, not really listening.

It was good that Christy and I had different lunch periods. I didn't want to see her. I'd deleted the text messages she'd sent me since my arrest. She said her dad didn't want us to talk anymore.

I was glad when it was finally ninth period, even though math class seemed to take forever. I was tired of polynomials and other stuff that would be useless in life. Math had the ability to slow time. The clock always slowed to a crawl in ninth period, the last period of the day.

Mr. Allen, my math teacher, was thin, old, and bony. I could almost see right through him, like he was transparent. He had a ring of white hair that went around the side of his head and eyes that were constantly watching you. I heard he was the veteran of some war—probably World War I.

Highland Middle School had been built back in 1922.

It looked kind of like a castle on the outside, but new on the inside. It had heating but no air-conditioning, and teachers wouldn't turn on the fans because they would just blow your papers around.

"Kevin, will you kindly share your thoughts on this problem?" Mr. Allen asked.

Hearing my name, I panicked and turned to the kid next to me for help.

"We're on num—"

"There is still a minute left in the period, Mr. Johnson. If you cut short every period by a minute, do you know how many minutes you'd waste in an entire school year?" he said, spewing out saliva while he spoke. I turned away to avoid it, which only made Mr. Allen madder.

The bell rang, and I was saved from another one of his boring lectures about how in his day, things were so much tougher and how kids these days have no discipline.

I wasn't a troublemaker, but I wasn't a suck-up, either. Ms. Grosnickle and I had had a few "conferences," as she liked to call them. She told my mom I had to watch my temper. I wondered if I was going to get called into her office because of the arrest. I hoped not.

I zigzagged around kids through the overcrowded hallways, bumping fists with my friends.

"What's up, Kev?" my friend Rich said as he slapped me five and walked by.

I don't know why some people ask what's up and then don't stick around for an answer.

Through the crowd, I thought I heard a voice call, "Kevin, wait up!" I wasn't sure, as the loud noises of the hallway made it difficult for conversation. I turned around. Calvin Anderson, my best friend, was behind me. He quickly gave me a playful dead arm.

"Hey," I yelled.

"When did you get out? Heard some stuff happened."

"Yeah, let's get out of here first."

We walked down the stairs and toward the exit, talking about what had happened at school the day I was gone.

Some of the really popular kids were hanging around near the front door. I don't really get popularity, because most kids who are popular are mean, and the rest of the kids don't even like them.

We burst out of the door. The fresh air felt good against my face.

The two of us walked home after school every day.

"What happened, man? People are saying a whole bunch of stuff and I don't know what to believe. You want to tell me about it?"

I sighed and looked in the other direction.

"Or not," Cal said as he looked at my expression.

"Listen, everyone's been looking at me weird and I just want to talk about something else, okay?" I said. "It's not that I don't want to tell you, I just don't want to tell you now."

"I didn't think you'd steal a car, Kev," Cal said. "What's gonna happen to you now?"

"I didn't really do anything terrible," I said. "Let's leave it at that."

"Yeah, okay."

Cal hadn't pushed it, even though I knew he really cared about me. Good.

"You're coming to practice tonight, right?"

"Yep, I'm looking forward to it. Might help clear my mind and stuff," I said.

"All right, I'll see you later," he said.

Our team, the Highland Raiders, had practice four nights a week and a game or a tournament on the weekend. It got cold playing at night later in the season, and the sun was almost down when I got to practice.

Cal, Shawn, and Ty, who was our center midfielder, were already there, practicing free kicks on Nick, our goalie, while a few of the kids were joking around on the sideline getting their shin guards on. I knew they'd be talking about the first State Cup game, which was going to be held the next week. I hoped they wouldn't be talking about me.

Most of the kids on the Highland school team also played on the Highland club team that Coach Hill had formed. Our team chemistry wasn't spectacular, with friends hanging out with friends more than acting as teammates. Kids would side with their friends in the group if there was a disagreement.

Coach Hill pulled up in his car, and we helped him carry the equipment to the field. He wasn't an easy person to like, but he was a good coach. Physically he was tough on us, and mentally he was even tougher. He'd make us run through cones during the winter until we threw up, which I did more than once.

He was always telling us, "You're not supposed to like me. I'm your coach. Sure, I want you to do well. Yeah, I care about you, but I don't want to be friends with you.

I have enough friends already."

As I was helping him set things up on the field, Coach pulled me aside. "Look, Kevin, I don't know what you did, or why you did it, but I do know that I'm not going to tolerate that sort of behavior. You're on thin ice with me, so step lightly. Do I make myself clear?"

"Yes, Coach." That could have been worse, I thought. He didn't say I couldn't play.

Coach blew his whistle and had us gather around. He started talking about our preparation for the State Cup, and I zoned out.

"Kevin, eye contact is not an option. It's mandatory." Coach gave me the eye and I thought he was going to get mad, but he didn't. Police sirens sounded in the distance, and a few kids instantly looked in my direction. That pissed me off.

"I think we can go pretty far this year as a team, but our midfield needs to get their act together. We can't just have good defense and forwards, 'cause the ball can't just magically go from one end to the other without going through the midfield."

Coach Hill had played professionally but had suffered a career-ending injury. He didn't like to talk about it, though. I wondered if it was hard, watching us play, while he walked with a limp. I heard he had been in a car accident. Now he was heavy, mostly bald, and wore a small goatee that made him look more like a pro wrestler than a soccer player.

We split our team up and played an eight-against-eight game at practices. We always started practice with one drill that Coach Hill thought was key. It was a mix of conditioning and dribbling. This was the part of the practice where guys regularly puked.

"You know what?" Coach Hill said after we completed the drill and guys were huffing and puffing on the ground. "I think we need to do that drill again. I didn't like the enthusiasm," he said, chuckling.

"From the beginning?" I groaned.

"No, first we're going to do the middle, then move to the beginning and then the end," Coach said sarcastically.

"That's what I thought," I mumbled.

"Of course from the beginning," Coach Hill yelled. "And Kevin, you can do it twice more. Let's go!"

That was Coach Hill for you. I guess you had to learn not to take him personally, but it was hard.

Coach Hill felt that most drills were a waste of time. He said the only way we were going to get better was to play games. "How do you think the guys from Latin America got good? They played in the streets with their friends every chance they got. By playing a game, you get conditioning, skills, and awareness."

Coach put me in at forward, and I knew he'd be keeping an eye on me. If I messed up at practice, he wouldn't start me in the tournament.

I remembered his words at our last practice, when I had come down the sideline and lost the ball.

"Kevin, it does no good if you can get to the goal but can't finish. You can dribble up to the goal all you want, but until that ball hits the back of the net, we're not going to win games." I knew Coach was right.

Ricky Sorin was Coach Hill's favorite player, and he put him in at the other forward position on our side. Ricky was full of himself and had a lot of confidence. He walked around like he was better than everyone else, strolling in late to practice and making a big deal of texting on his cell phone as if everyone in the world was trying to reach him. He got away with things that I knew the other guys on the team would have been killed for. He was good but not that good.

Someone passed the ball to me and I wasn't paying attention. It went between my legs. "What was that, Kevin?" Coach Hill yelled. "Get your head in the game!" That was impossible.

CHAPTER
05

The assistant DA called and said that he had spoken to McNamara and that it looked like he was going to press charges. If all McNamara needed was to get his car fixed, I knew that would have been a simple way out if Kevin's mom had had the money to pay for it. I knew I could have probably raised the money from the guys at the precinct if it wasn't outrageous, but I also knew that McNamara might have thought he had hit it rich.

I called Kevin and asked him if he would meet me after school, and he said he would. I also asked Paul Gross, my partner, if he would look up McNamara to see if he had a criminal record. He wasn't in any of the main files, but ironically, he had a mention in the tickler file on a letter I had written close to four years ago. I reread it before I left for the school.

12TH HIGHLAND COMMAND
EAST DISTRICT

To: Captain Jonathan Bramwell
From: Gerald Brown
D/O/R August 12, 2008
Re: Possible exploitation of workers
Status: Cessation of ongoing investigation

As per instructions we have terminated the investigation in the South Brunswick Park area. The investigation, involving four officers and myself, consisted mainly of interviewing, when possible, residents of the area, especially those who are recent to the community. Most of these are of Latino heritage with little or no English and might be illegal immigrants. The investigation was initiated on the suspicion that some of the new workers were being exploited by being employed at below minimum wages or were being forced to make kickback payments to an illegal agency.

The conclusions we came to are that while there is still a possibility of exploitation, it is very difficult to determine because of the closeness of the community and the fears of deportation. We did not investigate the immigration status of people in the community because that is not our jurisdiction. But the possibility of status violations did hamper our efforts for extensive interviews. It does appear that if there are abuses in South Brunswick, they are not extensive at this time. We can't, without more evidence, continue to devote manpower to this task but should keep an eye out for clues that would make a more thorough investigation pertinent. We should also create a tickler file of names of recently hired workers and the firms or individuals that employ them.

I would also like to point out the department's lack of Spanish-speaking officers. With the population of Latinos in Highland expected to rise, it may be good thinking to recruit among the Latino community.

The following people have been interviewed, some quite briefly, but their names should be recorded in the tickler file in case some other incident or complaint brings important information to the case.

Patrice Carabella
Petra Valeria Diaz
Charles Valente
Marta Molnar
Adamo family
Michael McNamara
Cristobalina Ibarra
Thomas Jones
A. Muchison

Respectfully submitted,

Gerald Brown

It was nothing important, and McNamara certainly didn't look as if he was into anything illegal. But he had mentioned that Kevin had been to his house, and I thought that maybe something had happened there that got McNamara pissed off.

When I arrived in front of the school, Kevin was wearing sweats and standing with a friend. The friend came over to the driver's seat window.

"You'd better cuff him," the kid said, smiling. "He's pretty good with his hands."

Kevin slid in beside me, and I waited until he fastened his seat belt before pulling away from the curb.

"I told my wife that I wanted to talk to you, and she invited us both for some milk and cookies," I said.

"That's pretty old-fashioned," he said.

I stopped the car and eased it over to the curb. "Look, Kevin, this case can go in a lot of—"

"I'm sorry."

"*Don't* interrupt me!" I said.

"Yes, sir."

"One of the things I've learned on this job is not to get myself involved with the people I arrest, their families, or even with the victims. The one reason—and get this straight—the only reason I'm dealing with you is that your father was something special. I wanted to ask you if anything had ever happened between you and McNamara to make him mad enough to cause you trouble down the line. But you're getting me mad every time you open your mouth."

"I'm really sorry, sir," he said. "I really am."

"Now do you want those 'old-fashioned' milk and cookies or not?"

"Yes, sir, I do."

Anger is not always a bad thing. When I was twenty, it helped get my adrenaline flowing and pulled me out of a few tight spots. At three years before retirement and five pills a day to keep my blood pressure down, anger was not a good thing.

I drove carefully home, parked the car in the driveway, and started for the house.

"So this is Kevin." Carolyn smiled. "I've heard a lot about you, young man."

We went in and I saw that Carolyn had put out cookies on the coffee table. She asked Kevin if he would prefer diet soda to milk.

"The milk is fine, thank you," he said, glancing in my direction. "Ma'am."

"Nice to have some manners in the house again," Carolyn said.

She got the milk and we sat down on the leather couch we had bought the previous Christmas. Carolyn smiled again and then said something about looking at the roast in the oven.

"So—did you do anything to piss McNamara off?"

"No."

"Did you and Christy have a fight that night?"

"No."

"Why don't I believe you?"

"I think cops"—Kevin shrugged—"deal with a lot of people who tell lies."

"And you always tell the truth, I guess?"

"Yeah, I— There was that one time when the gym roof leaked," Kevin said. "He was pretty mad then."

"When the gym roof leaked? Tell me about it."

"Christy kind of gets by in school," he said. "Early this year she was out a few days, and then she blew a test big-time. It was a Tuesday, and she got a call at school because of something and she left in a big hurry. She was pretty upset. They had to let her go, but the teacher wasn't happy. I saw that she had left her backpack. Between classes I called her and asked her if she wanted me to bring it by her house after school."

"Yeah?"

"Well, that would have been after school and then after soccer practice. It was raining, and we were supposed to have practice in the gym."

"But the roof leaked?"

"Right, so since gym was the last period that day, I finished gym and practice and went right over to her house. I got there a little before three. I was there for maybe two minutes when her father comes home and he hits the ceiling, yelling at Christy about why she has a guy over to the house in the middle of the day and asking her if she went to school, that kind of thing."

"You said she was called home. Was there a problem?"

"I didn't think it was anything big," Kevin said. "Her mother wasn't feeling good or something and wanted her to come home."

"He say anything to you?"

"Just wanted to know who I thought I was hanging out in his house. The veins in his neck were all bulging and stuff. I thought he was going to take a swing at me. Then Dolores told him I was only thirteen and he kind of calmed down. He told me he didn't want me in his house when he wasn't there."

"How did you feel about that?"

"I didn't care. He's got nothing going on in his house, anyway. Christy doesn't do anything. She has to make supper for him sometimes or go to the store."

"What does the woman who works for them do?" I asked.

"She's like the mother sometimes," Kevin said. "I practice my Spanish with her. My grandmother wants to talk to me in English all the time except when there are strangers in the house and she doesn't want to talk bad English."

"Someone in the department interviewed McNamara when we were looking into illegal hiring practices. Some of the legal workers who didn't speak good English were being underpaid, too," I said. "Nothing came of it."

"You think Dolores is illegal?"

"Do you?"

"That's like a policeman's answer," Kevin said. "You just turned that right around."

"I don't have any reason to believe she's illegal," I said. "McNamara looks pretty straight to me."

"Maybe he just doesn't like anybody in the world.

Some people are like that."

"Fortunately, not many," I said. "You been talking to the girl?"

"She said he doesn't want us speaking," Kevin said. "I think that's like those shows you see on television where the judge says that nobody is supposed to talk about the case."

"You like Christy?"

"No!"

"You had a fight?"

"No."

"You were driving in the car with her that night, Kevin." I spoke slowly for emphasis. "You just told me a story about how you brought her backpack to her house because she had left it in school. So what happened that you don't like her?"

"I mean, I like her, but I don't like her like I *like* her or anything like that," he said.

"You're not in love. You're just friends."

"Right."

"Best friends."

"Just friends," he said. "We went to preschool together."

"Who is your best friend?"

"Cal is now. My dad was. I'm not like him." He looked away.

"You don't have to answer this, of course, but why aren't you like him?"

"I have the right to remain silent?"

"Yeah, you have the right to remain silent," I said. "I didn't want to get into your personal business."

"My dad was good at a lot of things. You said that you learned not to get involved with criminals or victims. He told me he always worried about anybody he arrested. He would even pray for them at mass."

Kevin stopped talking, and I could see he was breathing more deeply, as if the emotions he was holding in were suddenly threatening to come to the surface. It came to me that this might be the source of his anger, the sarcasm, that they were all strategies to keep his emotions in check.

"You want another glass of milk?" I asked. "It's still old-fashioned, but I love it."

"You know my dad was better than me at soccer, too," he went on. "He said I'd be better one day and we would go into the backyard and play one-on-one. I always wanted to win, because he tried so hard to teach me that I knew he wanted me to win, to be as good as he

was. I have a pair of the shoes he played in. One day if I
ever get to play in a championship game . . . "

"You'll wear his shoes?"

"Yeah."

"You ever think of joining the force?"

"If I don't go to jail first," he said.

Carolyn came back into the room with two more
glasses of milk, and Kevin and I both turned them
down. Kevin asked if there was anything else I wanted
to ask him and I said no and we started for the car.

We didn't talk much on the way to his house. We
hadn't talked that much in my house, but I felt as if I
had seen the real Kevin for a change. There was a lot
going on in that head, a lot of good things. I was hoping
that if I could keep him out of trouble, they would keep
on going on.

When I got home, I was tired to the bone and was
glad of Carolyn's offer of hot lemon tea.

"Jerry, are you putting too much into this case with
Kevin?" she asked. "You've always made it a point to keep
your job away from your personal life, and now . . . "

"Now, I'm all into it?"

"Something like that."

"You know, when Judge Kelly first started talking

60

about working with kids, I started thinking about all the kids I've arrested over the years. Sometimes it had to be done, but in a way I've always felt that by locking them up, I was betraying them somehow. I think we need to give the kids a chance to show who they can be if they get the right support. They want to do the right thing, and sometimes they just need somebody who's there to show them what that right thing is. They'll still make mistakes, but maybe not the biggest ones."

"You're a good man, Jerry Brown," she said.

"And handsome, too," I said.

"I'll leave it at good," she answered. "And don't put the teabag on the end table."

CHAPTER
06

I knew that Dolores would be at Christy's house on Friday, so I headed over there after school to check things out. I just hoped that Christy's dad wouldn't be home. He was scary. Always mad at something, and always watching everyone like he was looking for trouble. I felt like I should try to help Sergeant Brown with his case, even though he didn't ask me to. I felt like I had a responsibility, since he was trying to help me. The whole thing was kind of interesting, too. Maybe even the kind of thing my dad used to do.

I felt kind of funny, though. I didn't want Christy to get into trouble because I was helping Sergeant Brown. That wouldn't have been right either. But what if Mr. McNamara wasn't paying Dolores what he should have been?

I rang the doorbell once and was about to push it again when Dolores opened the door. Yes! I'd seen her a lot more than I'd let on to Sergeant Brown. I'd known her since she'd started working for the McNamaras a few years ago, and I liked her a lot. She called for Christy, and I heard a faint voice yell "One minute" from upstairs.

"How are you, Dolores?" I asked in Spanish.

She looked glad to see me. Dolores didn't speak much English, so she was always happy when I went over to Christy's house because then she had someone to talk to in Spanish. I followed her into the kitchen.

"I'm fine, Kevin. How's your family?" she asked. Dolores didn't know my mom or grandma, but she always asked about them anyway.

"They're doing fine—my mom is always working

hard at the doctor's office," I answered back in Spanish. "How's your family?"

"Well, you know, it's hard being away from them, but I do what I have to."

Dolores's family lived back in San Salvador. She was trying to earn enough money here to send back to her kids, who lived with their grandma.

"So who do you live with here? You live all by yourself?" I asked her.

"Yes," she said before turning sharply and crossing the small kitchen to the dishwasher.

"Would you like something to drink?" Dolores asked me.

Just then Christy came to the kitchen door.

"Kevin, what are you doing here?" Christy looked surprised. And worried.

"Let's go sit on the porch," I said, walking toward the hall. "Bye, Dolores."

Christy flipped her light brown hair and followed me out.

I felt really uncomfortable, and me snooping around didn't make it any better.

"How's your mom?" I asked, sitting down on the porch steps.

"Not good," she replied softly. She looked sad. It was the same sadness I had seen the night I was arrested.

"I'm sorry."

"It sucks that you got arrested. How was Bedford?"

"Not too bad, once you get past the terrible food, awful bed, and the gangs," I lied.

"You didn't . . . tell?"

"No."

It was weird seeing Christy after everything that had happened. Even though we were friends when we were really little. I felt so sorry for her, but I was kind of pissed off. I knew it wasn't her fault, but it wasn't my fault, either. And I was being blamed. Maybe my sneaking around sort of evened things out between us.

"One, two, three, Highland Raiders!"

I was nervous as we ran onto the field, ready to play our first State Cup game. Since Mom was at work, Sergeant Brown had driven my grandma and me to the game. He had called to see if I needed a ride and I told him I was going with Cal. Of course I ended up going with him.

I was happy to be a starter, and I was glad Coach Hill was still letting me play. I didn't want Sergeant

Brown to come to the game to watch me sit. I wasn't sure exactly how I felt about him, but I still wanted to impress him.

I had watched East Ridge practice before. They had dynamite uniforms. They were the kind of team that really looked good until they started playing.

"Every one of them is big," I told Sergeant Brown. "They look like tenth graders."

"Your team have a chance?" he asked.

Yeah, we had more than a chance. I could probably outrun anyone on East Ridge, but I didn't know how good their goalkeeper was.

We lined up in our 4-4-2 formation, with four defenders, four midfielders, and two forwards. I started at forward with Ricky. My stomach felt jumpy like it always did before every game. I didn't know how I was going to be able to run.

East Ridge started with the ball. The ref blew the whistle. They passed the ball back toward their defenders, and I immediately sprinted upfield to get into position. There was no sense in chasing after the ball while their defenders played with it in the back. I needed to conserve my energy.

They started off playing better than I expected. They were using their size to their advantage, and playing dirty, too. As soon as one of our players got the ball, he would be lost in a swarm of red. They were deliberately stepping on our guys and pushing us down with body contact. Our guys started hesitating to take on a player, so East Ridge would pass the ball right back to the player who sent it to them as soon as they got it. The ref called them on a few fouls, but not as many as he should have. My mind wandered back to the arrest, but I tried to stay focused.

I stayed on number 7, the last defender before their goalie, so if my team got the ball, they could play it over the defenders to me and I could run on to it. About fifteen minutes into the game, East Ridge received a corner kick. They immediately went into their set corner kick positions. Our team lined up in the box around the goal, matching up against their attackers.

"Cut the pushing and shoving!" the ref yelled.

I was getting into the game and forgot about my stomach.

The corner kick landed straight in the middle of the box. Cal jumped up and headed it out.

We were on the offensive. Alex, one of our two center midfielders, took control of the loose ball. The East Ridge defenders scrambled to get back. There was space for a pass, and I yelled for the ball between the defenders. I made sure I wasn't offside. Alex had great peripheral vision and saw me with my hand raised. The pass was beautiful, right through a hole between two defenders into the open field. I took off, sprinting past the other two defenders. It was just the goalie and me.

Low and into the corners. Nothing fancy, Kev, just fake in and cut out.

I slowed down as I approached the goalie, who had come out of his box. I faked a shot and took it outside to the right with the outside of my foot. I thought I had beaten him, when he dove down and grabbed the ball. I tried to kick it away from him, but he held on tight. I was so frustrated, I kept kicking the ball even though the goalie had his arms wrapped around it.

"Enough! Number thirteen, the goalie has possession of the ball," the ref said.

"C'mon, Kevin, at least get a shot off!" Coach yelled. I wanted to ask Coach Hill if he could come out on the field and do any better.

Another corner kick and an East Ridge player, taller than anyone on our team, went up and headed the ball into the net.

Losing 1–0. Coach sat us down.

"You're taking it to them and they're getting tired. You should use your speed to your advantage. They can't keep up with you. They had one lucky shot. You're terrible on their side of the field." Coach Hill was shouting. "We're getting some good shots set up but no one is finishing them!"

"C'mon, Coach, I got no help up top!" Ricky complained.

I could feel anger building up inside me. He was blaming *me* for *his* mistakes.

Coach ignored the comment. "Do you want to lose in the first round? You're sure playing that way. This is where you find out what kind of team you are!"

We had the ball in the second half. Ricky and I stood next to each other in the circle in the middle of the field at the halfway line. The ref signaled to make sure the goalies were ready and then he blew his whistle. I tipped the ball to Ricky, and he passed it diagonally to one of the outside midfielders, Shawn, who had sprinted up the field and gotten the ball. Shawn could shoot with accuracy from nearly anywhere on the field, farther than the rest of us. He played either left or right wing, racing down the sidelines and shooting if he had the open shot. If the defenders converged on him, he was great at passing the ball into the center. He was one of the most consistent players on the team, rarely turning the ball over. But this time, Shawn was easily outnumbered six to one and lost the ball.

"Keep possession!" Coach called out.

Their defenders started to pass the ball among themselves.

When you see a defender standing like a statue, waiting for the ball to come to him, you intercept it.

I saw my chance and took the ball a few yards away from the surprised defender's feet. I ran to the left corner of the field, looking to cross it in. I realized I didn't have enough power in my left foot to cross the ball all the way into the box, so I cut inside, knocking the ball square into the box. Ty, who had his hand raised calling for the ball, connected with it and volleyed it with ease into the bottom corner below the diving goalie. I rushed to Ty and gave him a slap on the shoulder.

"Nice pass, man," he said.

"Thanks, great goal."

"Nice work, Ty! Good job, Kevin. Kevin, next time you go in for the cross on the left, don't cut in, hit it with your left foot! C'mon, you should know better."

Soccer coaches always put a lot of emphasis on learning to kick the ball equally well with both feet. If there was an opportunity to use the left foot, they hated to see the player use his right. I was happy, and I shrugged his comments off. I really didn't care. I thought that was a nice cross. Why was he getting on my case when we just scored?

I glanced over at Sergeant Brown and Abuela. Sergeant Brown looked confused, but Abuela appeared to be explaining the game to him. She didn't seem to mind speaking English to him.

The momentum was shifting. We got possession of the ball again and I saw Ty driving forward. I motioned for him to pass me the ball. I saw the defender coming and shouted, "Man on!" but it was too late.

Their number 18 slid, feetfirst with his cleats up, into the backs of Ty's calves. He let out a sharp cry and collapsed to the ground in pain, then sat up, clutching his leg.

The kid spat on him. Ty got up and threw his fist right onto the kid's head. Number 18 fell down, bounced up, and punched him. Just as number 18 was about to land another punch on Ty's bruised face, I tackled him. While both of us struggled on the ground punching each other, several players from our team and theirs started a scuffle. Someone grabbed my legs and dragged me off number 18 while the ref was shouting.

It was Cal. I wrestled free from him. Number 18 was cursing at me. I landed a solid punch, right on his jaw. The force knocked him to the ground. The ref immediately ran between us. He started to yell at me, but I tuned him out. Both refs cornered me and gave Ty, number 18, and me all yellow cards. Then the ref took a red card from his pocket and raised it over my head. Sergeant Brown had his arms crossed and was shaking his head. He did not look happy.

Number 18 was still on the ground, writhing in pain. His coach ran over in a rage and shouted at me, "That kid should be suspended from this league!"

Coach Hill yelled, "Kevin, Ty, I don't care how much pain you're in, get off the field now!"

My bruised face hurt a bit. The pain would probably

go away soon, a lot sooner than the trouble I had caused would.

"Kevin, you could have just cost us the game, because of your selfishness and lack of control. Now we have to play down with ten men."

"I'm glad you're concerned with Ty's calf, Coach," I muttered under my breath.

"What did you say?" he asked as he turned to me and raised his eyebrows.

"I said I'm mad with this half's approach."

The red card took me out of the game and the next scheduled game as well. Even if we did end up winning this game, I would have to sit out the second round of the State Cup.

"This is why you're in trouble all the time! They could suspend you from the league!" Coach screamed. By helping my teammates, I had really let them down.

Even with ten players, our team dominated the second half, scoring twice. The other team knew the game was over with five minutes left in the second half. They played like it, too. At the end of the game, two kids on East Ridge were crying. Some didn't even shake hands with us. Number 18 gave me the coldest look I'd ever seen. He was rubbing his jaw.

"What happened back there?" Cal asked. "You looked crazy mad. Your veins were popping out and stuff, and when I saw you with that look you get when you're really mad, I knew you had lost it."

"I gotta protect my teammate, Cal."

"You can't play next game, right?"

"I know, but that kid got what was coming to him," I said.

"Hey, if soccer doesn't work out, you'd be a good boxer."

I gave Cal a playful shove.

"You're a beast, man. You nailed that sucker," Nick said, giving me a high five as he passed by.

The ref asked my coach for my card. I would only get it back after the next round.

I heard the ref say, "Kids like number thirteen should be banned from playing soccer."

I had chosen number 13 because I wanted to show everyone that I didn't believe in bad luck, but now I wasn't so sure anymore.

Coach gathered us around him for a postgame talk. "You played much better in the second half, but if you play like that the next game, you guys will lose. You shouldn't be happy with your performance. They let you win. And we can't have players losing their heads. That's unacceptable behavior." He looked right at me and then at the team. "You shouldn't be rewarding Kevin for his behavior by saying it's cool. You should be discouraging it."

Sergeant Brown looked betrayed. I felt like I had let him down. And now I had an even bigger problem. I wondered if he was going to call Judge Kelly and recommend that he send me back to juvie.

CHAPTER
07

Soccer was hard to follow. The teams were going down the field at a slow pace for a while, then everything would speed up, maybe there would be a try for a goal, and then the whole thing would go the other way. Somehow Kevin was always in the middle of most of the plays and all the confrontations.

After the game, I took Kevin and his grandmother home. When we reached the house, I told him to see his grandmother to the door and come back to the car.

Kevin returned and got in. "We going someplace?" he asked.

"No, I just wanted to tell you a story," I said. "About four years ago, I was working over on Evergreen Avenue. You know where they were going to build that park?"

"It's got that little pool for kids?" Kevin asked.

"Right. Anyway, there was an abandoned building across from the park and we were told that some crackheads were using it to sleep in. I went in and didn't see anything on the first floor. I called up the stairs to see if anyone was in the building. No answer.

"My partner went to the rear of the building and I headed up the stairs. I didn't expect any trouble. I looked around on the second floor and it looked empty. I was looking for trash, empty food containers, things like that. I thought I saw something in a corner and put my flashlight on it, and all of a sudden, I heard a gunshot. I turned and saw this jerk with a pistol in his hand. He fired again and I drew my weapon. He tried to shoot again, but his gun jammed and he threw it at me.

"I told him to hit the ground, but he took off running toward the back of the building. I thought he might be going for another gun, but I saw him head toward the window. I got to the window and saw him climbing down the fire escape. I was pretty sure I recognized him. We picked him up two days later. You got all that?"

"Yeah, I guess," Kevin answered.

"I could have shot the guy when his gun jammed and he was still pulling the trigger. I could have shot him when he started to run. I could have shot him as he climbed down the fire escape. But even though I would have been justified in using my weapon, I didn't, for two reasons. One, I had more to lose than he did if the shooting was judged to be not justified. The second reason, and the most important, was that I held myself to a higher standard than that sucker. You get my drift?"

"I didn't shoot anybody."

"You hit a kid on the field today because he wasn't playing the way you thought he should have been," I said. "He set the standard and you sunk to it. Or was I seeing wrong out there?"

"You were watching—you weren't on the field!"

"And the refs, were they *just watching*, too? And was everybody out there wrong but you?"

"Sorry."

"Kevin, don't tell me you're sorry," I said. "Sorry is about forgetting to pick up the milk. Sorry is dropping a glass or making a mistake on a math test. Punching somebody on a soccer field, getting suspended from the game, is not sorry. It's called stupid."

"I guess I'm stupid, then."

"Was I wrong about you?" I asked him. "Maybe you're not a good kid who needs a break. Maybe you're a young man who thinks he can do whatever he wants as long as he thinks it's right."

"Look, I'm trying to do the right thing. I'm trying to do the right thing on the field and off. When you're sitting on one of the benches watching the game and you have time to . . . to . . . "

"To think about what should happen?"

"Yeah. If that ref had been watching all along, that wouldn't have happened."

"Life doesn't work that way and you're not going to be able to change that," I said.

"Whatever—the next time I'll just let them push us around and win the game easy," Kevin said. His voice had lowered. His head drooped.

"The thing to remember, Kevin, is that there won't always be a next time."

I motioned toward his house and watched Kevin start up his driveway.

On the way home I wondered again if we all had been wrong about Kevin. He acted too quickly on the field and had to be pulled away from the fight. Off the field, talking to him, he didn't seem like a hothead, but the punch he threw at the kid who fouled his team-mate looked hard and deliberate.

I got home and told Carolyn what had happened.

"Are you telling me that you never got into a fight at his age?" she asked.

"I got into fights when I couldn't avoid them," I said. "But this kid has an exaggerated sense of right and wrong. This team they were playing outsized them and they were going to use their muscle to win. Nothing wrong with that as long as they kept within the rules. Kevin's coach was yelling at his team to use their speed. But when this one player got a little dirty, Kevin went right after him. It wasn't pretty."

"Maybe it was because of all the tension he's under."

"Why do women always have to make excuses for chil-dren?" I asked. "If he was wrong he was wrong. Period."

"Now who's being belligerent?"

"If you say so," I answered.

I wasn't going to let Carolyn draw me into an argument. No matter what I said, she wouldn't budge off her position and we both knew it, so there was no use in even continuing the conversation.

"Did you at least leave him on good terms?" she went on.

"Carolyn, I don't want to discuss this anymore."

"Was your father as stubborn as you are?"

I picked up the remote and clicked on the news. I saw there was a traffic tie-up on Route 4 near Teaneck. They had an officer explaining how some college kids had rigged a motor to a couch and tried to drive it along the highway.

"It broke down a quarter of a mile before they got to Fairleigh Dickinson," he explained. "That's apparently where they were headed."

"You have an excuse for those idiots?" I asked Carolyn.

"No, your honor!" she answered.

We sat around for an hour watching television, and she was clearly being stubborn by not speaking to me. I was thinking of going up to bed when the doorbell rang. Carolyn answered it and came back quickly.

81

"There's a contrite young man to see you," she said.

I got up and went to the door. Kevin was sitting on the top step.

"How did you get over here?"

"Bike," he said, pointing to my front lawn. "Twelve and a half minutes."

I looked and saw his bicycle on its side. "What's up?"

"I know you were mad at me for fighting today," he said. "And I guess I was pretty mad, too. But I was wondering if you could do me a favor. Christy called when I got home. She said the transmission on the car wasn't working and her father thinks I messed it up. I don't think I did, but he was saying that he hoped I got five to ten years."

"You won't get that long as a juvenile," I said. "Not with a clean record."

"I thought maybe . . . you know, if you talked to him, you could convince him that I'm not that bad a guy," Kevin said. "Christy thinks he's mad at her, too."

"Maybe when your team is playing again and you can't play, we'll go over to his house and talk to him," I said.

He looked down at his hands. "Sergeant Brown, it'll

kill my mom if I have to go to jail," he said.

"Did you ever talk to him yourself?" I asked. "Tell him you're sorry?"

"He won't listen."

I sat down next to Kevin.

"Did he ever hit the girl?"

"Christy? I don't know."

"You don't know or you don't know if you want to tell me?" I asked.

"I don't think he hits her," Kevin said.

"I'll have to check with my commanding officer about speaking with him again," I said. "It can't look as if I'm putting any pressure on a citizen not to press charges if he wants to do it."

"Okay. I'm just pretty worried," he said. "And I don't really know anyone else to turn to. I don't think the lawyer is going to impress him."

"You need to be getting home," I said. "And call me so I know you're home safe."

"Okay." Kevin got up and straddled his bike. "Oh, yeah, I asked Christy how much they pay Dolores. I told her you were thinking of hiring a maid."

"Me having a maid is a funny idea," I said. "My mother

used to be a maid. Did Christy tell you how much they pay her?"

"They don't pay her," Kevin said. "They pay the agency she works for."

"Agency?"

"Yeah, she works for some kind of agency—Greenville Services—something like that—and Christy's father pays the agency and they pay Dolores. You want me to try to find out how much they pay her?"

"No! Look, Kevin, this isn't some soccer game with kids your age." I went over to where he was sitting and put my hands on the handlebars of his bike. "There might not be anything to this or it could be something that gets sticky in a hurry. I need you to promise me—absolutely promise me that you won't do any snooping around without me. This could get dangerous. Can you look me in the eye and make that promise?"

"Sure. I won't do anything if you don't want me to," he said.

I had interviewed a thousand people in my career. I could tell by their eyes when their minds went racing to what they should do or say next. Kevin's eyes shifted quickly down to the ground and away.

"Don't even ask Christy anything else," I said. "You understand that?"

"I understand it," he said, his fingers drumming nervously on the side of his bike.

"Okay, you go on home now," I said. "And call me when you get there. I'll think about talking to Christy's father again. I'm not making any promises, but I'll think about it."

"Okay, and thanks."

I watched him take off on the bike. He was in good shape and the bike sped down the street and onto the avenue in less than a minute.

I got back and Carolyn had two pieces of cake on the table.

"Why didn't you invite him in for cake and milk?" she asked.

"I don't want him out when it gets dark," I said.

"Everything all right?"

"I don't know. His eyes didn't look right," I answered.

"What's that mean?"

"I told him I didn't want him snooping around that alien worker case because it might be dangerous," I said. "The eyes on a kid his age should have got wide as soon as I mentioned danger. His got narrow and were darting from side to side. He was already thinking about what he was going to do next."

CHAPTER
08

Watching my team win their second State Cup game without me was agonizing. The score against Oakfield was 4–2 in our favor, and we were in control the whole game. I almost felt like I wanted my team to lose just to show them how much they needed me—even though I knew it wasn't right to think that way. In my mind I kept replaying the first game and what had put me on the bench. I hated players who played dirty, who didn't have any respect for the game. But now that I was sitting, I wished I hadn't lost my temper. I was getting myself into too much trouble. I thought about the story Sergeant Brown had told me about how he hadn't shot the man with the gun.

Sergeant Brown came over twice after school to check on me. It was a little awkward, because the other kids would spot him first and point him out. Some of them called him my "keeper." Since he didn't know anything about soccer, I took him out on the field and tried to show him how to dribble. He was slow and really not that well coordinated, so it was a tough job. In the end I got stuck full of thorns from trying to retrieve Sergeant Brown's awful passes from the bushes.

"So how's the case you've been working on?" I asked him when I came back with the ball. "The one with the workers we talked about the other day."

"It's not really active. We don't have many leads, and no one's willing to talk to us," he answered as he kicked the ball once again into the bushes.

"What about Mr. McNamara? Have you tried talking to him? You have lots of things to talk to him about."

"One of our officers tried to talk to him about it a few years ago. He wasn't very cooperative. When I tried talking to him about your case, I didn't get very far. Maybe I'll go see him again."

"Well, good luck. He's pretty tough," I said. Sergeant Brown's pass landed the ball right at my feet. Maybe we were getting somewhere.

Friday. Sergeant Brown was trying to help me and I needed to find a way to help him. I took a series of deep breaths as I crouched behind a thick bush on the side of Christy's house. I thought that Dolores probably wouldn't have enough money to buy a car, so following her home on foot would be easy. Then I could give Sergeant Brown Dolores's address, and he could go and interview her.

I knew Sergeant Brown might get mad over what I was doing, but how else could I help him? And I wanted to help Dolores, too. Once I explained it to him, he would understand. Maybe he would even thank me!

Christy's house was in a good neighborhood. The houses were neat and well-cared for. I thought they probably cost more than the house that my family lived in.

I waited behind the bush for an hour. I was growing impatient when, around five o'clock, I saw Dolores close

Christy's front door, lock it, and walk down the steps. I pulled up the hood on my sweatshirt.

Following Dolores was easy. I kept a good distance between us, and when she would turn a corner, I would immediately speed up until I could see her again.

I had been thinking about what Sergeant Brown had said about people with Hispanic backgrounds being exploited, and it bothered me. I knew I wouldn't want my grandmother being cheated in any way. Or my mom, either. What if I was back in Colombia and my mom was working here to support the family, just like Dolores? I didn't like people playing dirty. It didn't matter whether it was on or off the field—except this time I could do something about it. I knew why Dolores worked at Christy's house, but even that didn't make a difference if they weren't paying her enough.

I watched as Dolores stopped at a small grocery store. She made a few purchases and bought a newspaper. She walked slowly, and I could see her easily from a block away. I wasn't sure what I would learn that could help Sergeant Brown, but I was getting an idea of how she lived. As we walked,

I saw more and more children playing in the street. Men sat on milk crates outside the shabby tenements. The neighborhood no longer looked familiar to me. It was starting to get dark, and my mom would probably be worried if I wasn't home when she got there. Abuela would already be looking at the clock. I was debating whether to turn back when Dolores stopped at an old brick apartment building. It was run-down.

Dolores lived far enough away from Christy to have taken a bus, but she had walked the entire distance.

She opened the door with a key. I wanted to know which apartment Dolores lived in. I knew if it had a slam lock, I'd have to hurry. I sprinted forward and stuck my foot inside just as the door was closing. I listened for a few seconds before pushing the door open. The hallway was empty and quiet. I listened for footsteps and heard light steps just on the floor above and then the sound of keys opening a lock. I waited for a moment and then tiptoed up the stairs. I stopped on the second-floor landing just in time to see a door close behind Dolores. I peeked at the door. Apartment 2C. I listened at the door and could hear people speaking in Spanish.

I quickly ran down the stairs and out into the street. I felt good, as if I had scored a goal, but it was going to be a long walk home and I was going to be in trouble . . . again.

Wednesday. Game day, third round of the State Cup, and a call from Sergeant Brown. He didn't sound happy.

"Kevin, I'm sorry, I'm not going to make it to your game today," he said, letting out a sigh. "I'm having lunch with my in-laws."

"You don't like them?" I asked.

"It's just a family obligation," he said. "Look, Kevin, I don't want to hear from your coach or anyone else, and I sure don't want to have to call Judge Kelly."

"I've got it under control, sir," I said. I was sorry that I wouldn't see Sergeant Brown. I wanted to show him that I could play without losing my cool. I also wanted to give him Dolores's address in person, so I could see his face. Then he could go interview her and maybe whoever she lived with. I'd give it to him the next time I saw him.

I filled up three bottles with ice water from the fridge, grabbed a few pieces of toast, and ran upstairs.

"*¿Abuela, dónde están mis medias?*" I asked Abuela where my socks were.

I looked in my top drawer, where Abuela said she put them. As I pulled the socks out, I glanced at myself in the mirror above my dresser. I was starting to get a lot taller and more muscular, really fast. I was going to be tall like my dad, with the same green eyes, but with darker skin and black hair like my mom.

I went to my closet and reached all the way to the back, where I kept an old shoebox. I opened it and took out a pair of worn-out size twelve soccer cleats. Pretty soon they would fit me.

It was a cool and breezy October day. A few trees were starting to turn color, and some had already started dropping leaves on the ground. The game started at twelve thirty. Coach wanted us to be there at eleven. He said that the half hour before team warm-ups was for bonding and building team spirit.

Calvin's mom drove me to the game. Abuela was busy doing housework. My mom promised to take a day off from work if we made it to the semifinals.

We had a home game again. Our team chose a shady spot. I sat beside Cal, leaning against a tree.

"The Merredin Mustangs. What do you think, Cal?"
I said.

"We can beat them," he replied. "Remember, we played them once last season, but you missed that game. We only lost because the ref blew a call. Besides, our team wasn't as good as it is now. They've got a few good players, a little weak on the offensive side, but they make up for it with their defense."

"They got anybody special?"

"You see that kid over there?" Cal said, pointing to a far corner of the field at number 4. "He's a defensive monster," Cal continued. "Travis something—I forget his last name. He plays dirty, really dirty. He was the one that got suspended for punching that kid in the face last year down at the Baltimore tournament. The kid's face was all bloody and they had to take him away in an ambulance. Do you remember him?"

I did.

Coach Hill walked over to us. "All right guys, time for warm-up. Put your shin guards on and lace up your cleats."

We started with a light warm-up, jogging around the

field a couple of times and then stretching after the jog. Then Coach had the team sit down while he gave the lineup. He pointed to Nick as goalie and ran off the defenders, but I was waiting for him to name the forwards.

"Ricky and Robby are going to start at forward."

Cal and Shawn shot glances at me. I looked at them and rolled my eyes. I could feel the anger rising in me.

I had been expecting to hear the name that hadn't come. Mine. Other kids looked back at me. I looked away.

When the game started, I sat on the cold bench. I could see right away that Ricky was getting dominated. He couldn't handle Travis. He was getting intimidated, and beaten to the ball. As soon as Ricky received the ball, Travis would push him with his shoulders down. If Sergeant Brown had been at the game, I'd have had to explain that this was considered a fair move. Travis was built like a tank, and he acted like one. But I could have handled him, if Coach had put me in.

But Merredin's forwards couldn't penetrate our defense. One of their forwards hit a powerful shot from outside the box and Nick dove for it. The post rang as the ball hit it dead on and bounced off. Nick got up from the ground and recovered the ball.

That kid can kick, I thought.

Ricky was chickening out big-time. He would give Robby the ball as soon as he received it to avoid getting hit. Travis picked up on this and was double-teaming Robby. Robby was an okay player. He was always tripping over himself and was a little clumsy and uncoordinated, running with his arms flailing, but he tried really hard so nobody minded. We all liked Robby.

Two minutes later Travis and another defender switched guys, which put Travis on Robby. As soon as Robby got the ball, Travis nailed him right in the calves. He tumbled to the ground, clutching his legs.

"Kevin, get ready!" Coach yelled. He walked onto the field to check on Robby.

It's about time, I thought. I jumped up from the bench and tucked in my shirt. Now I'd show him. I had to score. I was *going* to score.

Robby limped off the field with Coach, and I ran into position. I knew that if I could pull this off, it would have to be with my speed.

Travis switched back to defend Ricky. The first time I got the ball, I dribbled toward a defender, who knocked the ball away. I ran back and tackled him from behind.

The ref blew his whistle.

"Number thirteen, watch the tackles from behind!" he called to me.

Travis switched from Ricky over to me and gave me a grin.

Ty passed me the ball. Ricky was wide open. I wasn't going to pass the ball to Ricky, because I wanted to show Travis and Coach that they were wrong about me. I took the ball and went at him. I knew what I wanted to do.

The move, if you do it right, works and looks great. If you screw it up, you look like a fool.

I couldn't let Travis get a good look at the ball. I put my right foot on top of the ball, then quickly turned my back and spun the ball with my left. I heard a bunch of oohs and aahs from the spectators. Travis came right behind me and slid into me, hard. I fell to the ground, and the ref blew the whistle. He held up a yellow card.

"If I have to warn you again, you'll be gone, number four!"

Travis cursed just loud enough for me to hear him.

I got up and was about to clock Travis but stopped

myself in time. I wasn't going to go there again. I thought of Sergeant Brown's reminder. There was too much at stake for me to lose my temper. I walked away and got into position.

The ref gave our team a free kick. Cal placed the ball down. He raised his hand as his foot connected with the ball. No one even touched the ball as it glided into the net under the diving goalie.

I looked at Coach while the rest of the team cheered. He was smiling—an expression we'd rarely seen since the game had started.

Next possession we got the ball and I went to the outside of the field, the flank, to receive it. Ricky was open, but my plan was to run down the field and then cross the ball in to Ricky for the goal. I breezed by everyone and went toward the goal. I wanted this goal for myself, but Ricky was on the other side of the goalie, running with a defender. I drew out the goalie, taking the ball almost out of bounds next to the side of the net before I made a short quick pass with the outside of my right foot to Ricky, who tapped it into the net with his toe.

Ricky and I slapped hands and jumped up, bumping our chests together, as the rest of the kids surrounded us.

"Terrific plays, guys, I like the teamwork! Kevin, way to draw the defender out for the assist. Good unselfish play!" Coach yelled.

We went on to win the game 3–1. It felt great.

CHAPTER
09

"Carolyn, I started this little adventure with a clear head and as much patience as I could muster," I said, looking at my half-finished breakfast. "Now my head isn't clear, my patience is gone, and this kid is jeopardizing my job."

"Jerry, how is Kevin—"

"If something had happened to him while he was playing Sherlock Holmes yesterday, it would have looked bad on me because I'm supposed to be keeping an eye on him," I said. "What I think I want to do is to pack it in. I'll just call Judge Kelly and tell him that this kid needs to be in custody."

"You went into this thinking that these kids don't always think things through, but that they deserve a chance," Carolyn said. "Isn't that right?"

"I'm going to talk to him today," I said. "And if one answer is shaky, I'm finished with him."

"Is he coming here?"

"No."

I knew I didn't want to bring Kevin to the house or any other place where we would be sitting down talking like normal people, because the boy wasn't normal. He had called me at half past eight, all excited, to tell me that he had followed the woman who worked for the McNamaras to her house and into her building.

If there had been something fishy going on, if what we had suspected about illegal aliens being mistreated was true, he might have found himself in a situation he couldn't have come close to handling.

Human Resources had posted a notice of state physicals down at Sea Girt. It was a bit of a trip, but I knew I needed time to cool off. I called Buddy Wright and asked if I could bring Kevin down and let him take a physical.

"He a good candidate?" Buddy asked.

"No, he's just a kid, but I want to bust his chops a little," I said.

"Bring him over," Buddy said.

There hadn't been any mistaking my anger when Kevin called. The conversation had started with his bubbling over about how clever he had been to trail Dolores from a distance and had ended with me yelling into the phone. When I picked him up in front of his house, I just unlocked the door and didn't even look at him.

We drove for ten minutes with him leaning against the passenger's side door, as far away from me as possible. When we reached the Garden State Parkway, he finally spoke.

"We going to juvenile prison?"

"What were you thinking?" I asked. "Just tell me what you were thinking so I can try to wrap this old head around it."

"I was thinking . . . "

"You *weren't* thinking!"

"I thought I was thinking that you were trying to help me," he said. "You were telling me good stuff about how to stay out of jail and you talked to Mr. McNamara. I just wanted to do something that was useful to you."

"By playing junior detective and putting yourself in danger?" I asked. "Or by alerting anybody who might have been doing something illegal that the police were watching them?"

"I thought you said that the investigation had ended."

"If there's possible criminal activity going on, we don't stop investigating until we know it's *not* going on," I said. "That shouldn't be too hard for you to understand."

We pulled off the Garden State and took 34 into Sea Girt. I knew being mad didn't help anything, but I was furious with Kevin. I parked and he followed me into the front door of the Sea Girt Barracks.

I signed in and found Buddy in the gym. He and his staff were putting some applicants for state trooper through their physicals. I told Buddy what I was facing with Kevin.

"Put him on the line," Buddy said. "Let's see what he's made of."

I knew Buddy was trying to give me a chance to calm down, so I motioned for Kevin to get on the line of men and women trying out for the next rookie class.

"And after every station, come back over here and talk to me!" I said.

Kevin looked a little confused, but he joined the first line.

The police department physical consisted of four timed tests. The first one consisted of push-ups. Each candidate was given two minutes to do as many push-ups as possible. The minimum standard was eighteen.

"He looks like a nice kid," Buddy said as we watched the guys doing push-ups.

"Nice, but clueless," I said. "The only reason I'm around him is that his father fell on duty."

"Not state?"

"Highland."

I watched when it was Kevin's turn. He got into position, and when the signal was given I could see him pumping furiously. He did twenty-seven push-ups, his face turning a bright red from the exertion. He was breathing hard when he came over to where I was sitting on a fold-up chair near the wall.

"Talk!" I said.

"I want to be useful," he said, trying to catch his breath. "Really, I do. About six months after my dad died, some people came over to the house. One of them was my cousin Jorge. I think he was my cousin; maybe he was just a friend of the family. He said I was the man of the house. He asked me if I had a job. I didn't. I was thinking about getting a part-time job to help out."

"Group B, line up!" a cadre was calling.

Kevin looked around. "They said I was in Group B," he said.

"So what are you doing over here?"

I watched as he ran over to his group. The task was sit-ups, and I watched as a man in his thirties struggled to reach a sitting position, The cadre timing him looked down at the candidate, holding the clock so that the man could see it. The cutoff was twenty sit-ups, and it was clear the guy wasn't going to make it. He didn't, and you could see the disappointment. If you failed one of the cutoffs, you were automatically disqualified for the state police.

Kevin was young and light and started the sit-ups as he had the push-ups, in a furious spurt. He slowed down at the end but he made the cutoff. He walked back to me.

"Next time, run back to me!" I said. "Talk!"

"There was a poem by an Irish writer—my dad was Irish—that said that when things went really wrong, the bad people would be active and the good people would sit around and do nothing." Kevin looked around the barracks, and I could see he was feeling bad. "He used to say to me that all he ever wanted was for me not to be somebody who sat around and did nothing when there was something that needed to be done."

"Even if you had to do something stupid?" I asked.

"He mentioned . . . that there were a thousand excuses," Kevin said. "All you had to do was to put your hand out . . . "

"You remember the name of the poem?" I asked.

"'The Second Coming,'" he said. "By Yeats."

Group B was being called again, and Kevin took a deep breath and went back to where the cadre was standing with the stopwatch. There was a group of people gathering along the paneled walls of the gymnasium. They had failed the tests and were already on their way home. The test wasn't that hard for youngsters, I thought. It was good to weed them out.

The third test was the mile-and-a-half run. I was pretty sure that Kevin could do it. They took everyone outside and put them into two groups. One group of about fifteen would start first and then the other group would start two minutes later. They had to do the mile and a half in no more than 14.25 minutes.

I watched the first group take off and then saw Kevin go to the side of the track. It looked for a minute as if he was going to vomit, but then the cadre whistled for his group to go and he started.

It was strange to think of him running around with all those wild thoughts in his head, all that extra weight. I could imagine him sitting on the edge of a field with a father who taught him how to kick a soccer ball, who gave him little speeches about life, and even read him a poem that defined the role of a good human being. For all the world could see, there was simply a skinny kid with a temper running around the track with the older people, his long strides slightly more graceful than theirs, his body a lot less muscular but still growing, but inside there was a young man stumbling toward an uncertain future with a boldness that sometimes wasn't clear even to him.

He raced back and I saw the sweat on his forehead and brows. The kid was in good shape.

"Make sure to drink some water before the next event," I told him.

He went to the cooler, lined up behind two other guys gasping for air, and took a drink.

"It might not seem like it, but I can handle myself," he said.

"Against what?"

"I'm doing okay here," he said, looking over his shoulder at some of the candidates taking the physical.

"You're doing okay because there aren't any bad guys here, Kevin," I said. "These are guys who don't have a choice but to play by the rules. Once you leave this gym, all the rules are out the window. If they weren't, you wouldn't need young adults in the peak of physical condition to keep order.

"Talk!"

Kevin looked around as if something was going to pop up and give him a clue. "I thought what I was doing was right," he said. "At least I didn't think I was doing anything wrong."

"Does this affair have anything to do with Dolores?" I asked.

"No, I just thought I was helping you—"

"If I want your help, I'll ask for it," I said. "You were helping Christy?"

He shrugged. "Now I don't know who I was helping."

"You saying you can't talk to me?" I asked. "Or you saying you won't talk to me?"

"If I knew exactly what . . . what to say, then I would say it," Kevin said. "Do you always know what to say?"

"No, but I always know when I need to be talking to somebody besides myself," I said.

The last test was a seventy-five-yard run through a small obstacle course.

"You don't have to do this one if you don't want to," I said. "We can go home now."

"I'll do it," Kevin answered.

"Why?"

He bit his lip as he looked around. "I think I can handle it," he said.

I sat down and watched as Kevin lined up with the others. The course wasn't that long, only seventy-five yards, but there were turns and railroad ties that had to be negotiated. The candidates were proving that they had the stamina and coordination to run after a culprit and catch him in 19.5 seconds. The first guy who started off did it too quickly and fell, sliding into one of the cones he was supposed to negotiate.

Kevin looked up at me and I gave him the thumbs-up sign. I thought he could handle it too. He did.

I had a few words with Buddy and he complained about the level of applicants he was getting. For as long as I've known Buddy, he's been complaining but still turning out good officers.

The ride home was different from the ride down to Sea Girt. I was still riding with a thirteen-year-old, but he wasn't a stranger anymore.

"Can I trust you?" I asked when we reached his house.

"Yes, sir."

"I hope so," I said. "What it will mean—me trusting you—is that you've finally learned to trust me and the rest of the world. I'll be talking to you."

"Sir?"

"Yeah?"

"Thanks."

CHAPTER
10

I closed Sergeant Brown's car door and walked up the driveway. It was dusk. The sun had all but disappeared below the horizon, creating an eerie combination of shadows and light. I didn't realize I would be putting Sergeant Brown's job in jeopardy. I just wanted to help him. And Dolores. I thought Sergeant Brown would understand what I was doing, but now I was in trouble. Again.

Mom and Grandma were in the den, watching an old

DVD of *Betty La Fea*, a Colombian soap opera. I could hear them laughing. I tried to sneak past the door. But my mother's mom senses kicked in.

"So how was it?" she asked without even turning around.

"Fun," I said, starting up the stairs. I wasn't about to tell her Sergeant Brown almost lost his job because of me and I might be sent back to juvie.

"Come sit with us," Mom said, making room for me on the sofa.

Living with two women was hard. All I wanted to do was go and play video games upstairs. They just didn't understand me.

Reluctantly, I plopped down on the sofa.

"What did he say?" Mom asked, patting my back.

"He said that I was a bright athletic young man who would make a good police officer."

"Is that all?" Abuela asked.

"More or less," I said.

I wasn't lying; I just wasn't telling the whole truth. I thought it probably would be better to leave out the "reckless, loves to lie, sneaky, a car thief, and will probably spend the rest of his life in jail if he doesn't get himself killed within the next few days" part.

There was an awkward silence.

Mom paused the DVD. "I know it's been hard for you the past couple of years," she said.

Betty's face was frozen in the middle of her conversation, her eyes closed behind her thick-rimmed glasses, her mouth wide open, braces showing. It was no secret why the show was called *Ugly Betty*.

"Are you feeling a little bit better?" Mom said. "I still can't understand why you stole that car. You're not helping yourself by not talking to me."

"Okay," I said, and walked upstairs.

Later that night I lay looking up at my ceiling and the small vent centered above my bed. When I was little, I used to imagine that monsters were going to come out of that vent and eat me at any moment. My dad would run in and tell me it was all okay, never once getting angry at me. He even considered moving the vent, but then he'd have had to tear up the ceiling.

If only my dad were here now, I'd tell him everything that happened. He would have sorted things out. I know he would have. But it looked like I would have to get through this on my own. By trying to protect Christy, I was really hurting her. I bet that's what my dad would have said. And my mom, too, if I told her.

I was slowly drifting apart from Mom and Abuela. I could feel it. Conversations with them never used to be awkward, and now I knew they felt sorry for me all the time. I didn't want anyone feeling sorry for me.

Some kids at school said they hated their dads. They were lucky just to have a dad. Suddenly, I wasn't sure why, a wave of anger and resentment came over me. I punched my pillow, leaving an imprint of my fist on it. It took me a moment to cool down. God and I hadn't always seen things eye to eye. Or whatever God saw out of. I turned over, and the glow of the time on my digital alarm clock blinded me. My eyes adjusted just enough to see the picture behind it. Of my dad.

Cal and Tyler came over the following Friday. We hung out for most of the afternoon, then decided to get dinner in town. Cal wanted to look in some stores and stuff, and I just wanted to leave the house.

I washed up and changed my shirt before going.

"You're looking good." Mom fixed my collar when I came downstairs. "Just don't get into trouble."

As I was leaving with my friends, I heard Mom tell my grandma that soon the *chicas* would be all over me.

It felt good to get out of the house. This was what I wanted, just hanging and not worrying about being sent back to juvie or anything else.

"If I don't get my grades up, I might not be able to finish the soccer season," Ty said. "Mrs. Winters gave me an F in science. I think she loved failing me. I don't get why some teachers teach if they hate kids."

"Come on, I don't think she hates us," Cal said. "She probably just got picked on in high school or something and this is her revenge."

"You ever see her hand back a test with an F on it? She likes to watch kids fail. And do you see how big her Fs are? They cover the whole page!" Ty said.

We hung around the mall for over an hour. Other kids from school were there. We checked them out as they checked us out. A couple of kids there tried to start a fight with us. I thought we could take them, but I realized that wasn't a good idea.

I had almost forgotten about the arrest, being caught up in conversation and all, but not quite. No matter what, it was always gonna be in the back of my mind. Well, I hoped not *always*.

Then the three of us walked to Cold Stone Creamery on the other side of the mall. I got an icy blue Gatorade and Cal and Ty got ice cream. We sat outside the store at one of the aluminum tables.

"Yo, Kev, what's it like always being with that cop?" Cal asked. "What is he, a sergeant or something?"

"I guess he's all right," I said. "At first I thought he was just interested in getting information about the arrest, but now I'm thinking he actually wants to help me."

"That's cool," Ty said.

"But I really don't need any help," I said. "I'm fine and I just want to forget about it and get on with my life without him around all the time or having to answer a thousand questions."

"Yeah," Cal said. "Sure."

My friends looked at each other, but nobody asked me anything else. They understood I didn't want to talk about it.

For the next fifteen minutes we sat around trying to figure out which soccer teams in our area were the best. We decided that every team had a weakness and we'd have a chance to move on in the tournament.

"I think when we're on, we have the best team play," Ty said. "Our team play matches up with anybody's."

Cal's ice cream had looked so good that I decided to get some, too. As I returned with my cake batter and crushed Oreos, Cal nudged Ty and pointed across the mall.

"Hey, Christy and Emily are coming over here."

I didn't know why I felt a sense of panic, but my stomach knotted up just seeing Christy. I put my ice cream on the table and quickly went back into the store. I zigzagged my way through the crowd toward the bathroom. Inside, I splashed cold water on my face and dried it off with paper towels.

Sometimes going to school was boring, and there were times when even soccer practice wasn't that interesting. And I had been to the mall so many times, it wasn't the most exciting thing in the world, either. But now the boring parts of life were starting to look good. I knew Christy's drama was getting heavy on me, but I didn't know it could make me sick to my stomach.

I waited a few minutes until I thought the coast would be clear, but came out only to find that Christy was still talking to Cal. She saw me through the window, stopped her conversation with Cal, and entered the shop.

"Hey!" Christy said.

"What's up?" I asked, trying not to show that I didn't want to see her.

"How come you've been avoiding me?" she asked.

"I'm not . . . I don't know," I replied, looking at the floor. "I've been thinking—how come you let me go to jail and you never told the police what really happened? I haven't told anyone. I figured it was up to you."

"I'm really sorry, Kevin," Christy said. "You know how my dad is. If I say anything, it'll get back to him and I'll *really* be in big trouble. You know that."

"Is it always gonna be like this?" I asked. "I'm still the one in the most trouble."

"I hope not," Christy said.

Her eyes started to water up. I gave her a napkin. There was no way I wanted to have to explain to Cal and Ty why she was crying. I took her hand and we walked outside together.

Emily was hovering over my ice cream.

"Mmm. That looks good," Emily said. "Can I have some?"

"Sure," I said, and pushed it toward her.

I hoped her lipstick didn't come off on it. I hated that.

"Thanks. I'm thirsty, too," Emily said. "Can I have some of your drink?"

No, not the Gatorade! I thought.

I forced a smile and handed her the drink.

We left Cold Stone Creamery and started to walk home. Cal and Ty teased me about Emily having a crush on me.

"And my man just brushed her off," Ty said.

The air had gotten slightly colder outside, and I could see my breath rise up as I said good-bye. We split up and went our separate ways home. Going out with the guys had taken my mind off things. For a while.

"Wake up, sleepyhead—you're going to be late for your game!" my mom called the next morning. "I made you eggs and *chicharrón*. It's all ready for you downstairs."

"All right," I groaned. I was still sore from Thursday night's practice and had just woken up. I glanced at the clock; it read 11:00. "Mom, it's way too early."

"Kevin, humans are not nocturnal creatures. You

can't sleep all day and stay up all night."

My muscles were tight, and I struggled to bring myself out of bed. I got out of bed and walked drowsily down the stairs with my eyes half closed, following the smell. *Chicharrón*, bits of juicy pork still attached to the skin of the pig, was one of those things that sounded gross but tasted delicious.

The quarterfinals were about an hour and a half away at Fort Dix. I thought it was strange that the soccer fields for the State Cup quarterfinals, semis, and finals were right smack in the middle of a military base camp.

I fell asleep in Sergeant Brown's car on the ride to the field, and when I woke up, I didn't feel much like playing.

Getting my bag out of the trunk, I squinted across the complex to see which field we were playing on. Coach Hill's bald head and stocky figure were easy to spot, and most of my teammates were already there in their red and white uniforms.

"Get your head ready to play soccer!" I heard Coach yell as I approached the team. "We've made it this far, but so far, we haven't proven anything. The teams we've played have been all right, but not sensational. Today we have more of a challenge. The Oceanside Tsunamis are going to put up a fight. As for their defense, I think it's kind of slow and disorganized. Did you hear that, forwards? We have to take advantage of their defense to counteract their offense. Kevin, you and Ricky have to keep the pressure on their defense. I don't care if you get tired. Suck it up and keep the ball moving."

I was going to have to pace myself.

"The Tsunamis have some pretty good players who can be a threat to score at any given moment. Watch out for Santiago—he's their best player and one of the best in the state. Cal, if you don't you think you can handle his speed, I'll put Mike on him, or you guys can alternate if you need a break. He's going to be a handful, but remember, great teams win championships, not great players. We need team players to step up today, not individuals. Let's see how well you guys can handle pressure."

On the field we warmed up, and I was feeling better. I looked for Santiago and saw a kid who was taller than I thought he would be. He dribbled up and down the field, getting loose, and I could see he could handle the ball. I started feeling nervous, but it was a good kind of nervousness.

We huddled and got a last few words from Coach, and then it was time to play.

"One, two, three, Raiders!" we shouted.

I shot a look at Sergeant Brown on the sideline as I ran to my position and he smiled. I was glad he was there to watch me. Maybe it was a sign that he'd forgiven me for following Dolores.

The game got off to a slow start. The Tsunami offense controlled the ball. They were just playing it back and forth. They didn't score, but they didn't let us get the ball, either. I didn't have to run much since the ball was on the other side of the field most of the time. Not a good sign.

Slowly, our defense started to push them back and the game shifted to my side of the field. I was closing down the nearest defender as soon as they received the ball. I knew the defenders were feeling the pressure and were bound to make a mistake.

Suddenly, one of their defenders played a lax ball. It looked like it was rolling in slow motion. Shawn intercepted the ball at midfield. There was only a sole defender in sight. I was running in line with Shawn, having to hold my pace back a little so that I wouldn't be offside if he passed it to me.

We entered the eighteen-yard box. The defender backed down and then came toward Shawn, leaving me in the clear. Shawn lifted the ball with his foot up into the air toward me. I was ready for it and jumped so high in the air, it surprised me. Then I struck the ball with my head with such force, it whizzed right by the goalie, leaving him blinking. It was a slam dunk of soccer.

A roar came from the sidelines. Between high fives and pats on the back, I looked over at Coach Hill. He gave me a thumbs-up. I glanced at Sergeant Brown, who seemed to be enjoying himself.

I felt good. The field seemed clearer to me. After my goal I could feel my confidence grow. Once you score, you can afford to make mistakes. Playing without the fear of messing up lets you relax and really take your game to another level.

"We're playing well." Coach Hill was pumped at halftime. "But we have to keep fighting. They can get a quick goal and tie the whole game up! Don't get discouraged if they score. Just keep your composure and don't panic."

Less than five minutes into the second half, I scored my second goal. It was a long ball over the defenders' heads that I easily ran onto. I kicked the ball low toward the corners of the net and watched as their goalie turned his head too late. I thought, What is the point in having a goalie if he just stands there?

For the rest of the game, I was on cruise control.

Five minutes before the game ended, Coach Hill took me out. I didn't mind—I needed the break.

"Kevin, good job," he said, pulling me aside from the rest of the kids on the bench while he watched the game. "You have to display more discipline, but you're making smarter decisions and you handled the pressure pretty well—"

Coach was cut short by cheers from the other team's parents. Santiago had scored. I shook my head and returned to the bench.

I couldn't believe Coach had said that to me. Maybe Coach was right—maybe I just needed to be more responsible. I needed to be more aware, not just on the field but off the field, too. Sometimes adults didn't talk the same language as I did. Maybe Coach Hill didn't really want me on the bench, and I had figured out that Sergeant Brown wasn't going to send me back to juvie, either.

There were three more minutes left, and if our team could hang on, we would be one of the four teams in

the semifinals. Whenever there was a one-goal difference, the final minutes were agonizing to watch and
even more intense to play.

With thirty seconds to go, Santiago received a pass
from downfield. He was past our defenders!

Come on, Nick, I thought, you got this. Santiago
pulled a fancy move and passed the ball lightly into
the goal.

My heart sank. The game was going into overtime.

The sideline ref went over to talk to the main referee.
The main referee nodded and put up his hand, signaling the offside. Santiago was ahead of the last defender
when the ball was played to him. The goal didn't count!

Santiago and his teammates ran over to the referee
yelling, with their hands up in the air. The ref blew his
whistle to signal the end of the game.

We had won. We were going to the semis.

CHAPTER
11

"Ain't nobody likes a traffic cop, man!" The dude sitting on the bench, his wrist handcuffed to the railing, was wearing one of those old-fashioned undershirts with no sleeves. It was dirty and ripped down one side.

"So that's why you punched an officer of the law?" I asked him.

"I tried to explain to him why I was parked in the bus stop, but he wouldn't listen," the guy said. "Then he mouthed off at me. That's why I punched him."

"So what you can do now is to go over your explanation of why you were parking in the bus stop with whoever you're going to be sharing a cell with," I said. "Maybe he'll be more sympathetic."

I finished checking the paperwork, okayed it, and released the prisoner to the Detention Division. They sent over a young female officer to take the prisoner to the holding cells. I listened as he started in on her about how he couldn't afford a ticket on his salary and how the traffic officer hadn't even listened to him. He rambled on until he saw that the officer taking him down the hallway wasn't listening, either.

I got back to my desk and started straightening out the mass of papers that had unpiled themselves and were now covering most of the desk's surface.

"You got a call while you were gone," Paul said. "Pellingrino's office."

"The assistant district attorney? What did she want?"

"Said that they were looking to set a date for your boy's hearing," Paul said. "Her number's on your pad."

Rebecca Pellingrino was one of four Highland

ADAs. She was always straight with her dealings and didn't make any bones about the fact that she came down harder on violent crimes than she did on lesser offenses. I was surprised that she would be handling a juvenile case, though. I checked her number and dialed it.

"So—Judge Kelly says you have an interest in this case?" she spoke crisply, to the point.

"The boy's father fell in the line of duty," I said. "I hope we all have an interest."

"You speak to the victim?" she asked. "He's up and down on this. Some days it looks like he doesn't want to press charges and the next he's ranting and raving about juvenile crime. This week he asked me if the boy will get probation."

"He against that?"

"I don't think so," Pellingrino said. "I can't read him, really. But if he wants to push the case, we have to prosecute. We need to have a hearing to see if we're going to charge him with grand larceny or criminal mischief, a third- or fourth-degree felony. What does your calendar look like? Kelly has kicked it to Judge Lawler, and he's free all next month."

"How much time can you buy me?" I asked. "I'd like to see if there's anything more I can do."

"What's in it for me?"

"A double cappuccino and a bagful of Krispy Kremes."

"The sixteenth, ten A.M.."

"Two double cappuccinos and two bags of Krispy Kremes?"

"The sixteenth, ten-fifteen."

"Got it."

"Has he lawyered up?"

"His family has hired a lawyer, but they aren't that well off," I said. "Just some very scared people who want to keep their kid out of jail."

"That's the way the ball bounces, Brownie," she said.

"That's the way," I answered.

McNamara was still playing it close to the vest. His asking about probation for Kevin sounded as if he might not want to get the kid into too much trouble, but just enough for his insurance claim to go through. For McNamara, the idea of giving probation was just a slap on the wrist. For someone as young as Kevin, it could be a life-changing sentence. It would mean that he had pled guilty to a crime and might wreck his options with a college. The chances of the case getting to adult court were slim, but there was always the possibility. I needed to get busy.

The precinct caseload was pretty light— mostly burglaries around the new housing development and a break-in at one of the warehouses owned by the mayor, hence Captain Bramwell's interest. Paul and I were supposed to interview the warehouse manager that afternoon.

"You want to do it by phone?" Paul asked.

"Bramwell wants us to go down and make a showing, so it gets back to the mayor," I said.

"So let's do it," Paul answered.

"I want to get this kid's thing settled," I said. "You mind doing the interview alone?"

"What are you going to do?"

"I'm thinking of going over to that agency that Kevin mentioned—what was it?—Danville or something?"

"Greenville Services," Paul said. "I'll go with you. Let's pick up the kid in case they don't speak English."

"Good idea."

"Hey, Jerry, Kevin's growing on ya, isn't he?"

"No."

"Yeah, he is," Paul said, pushing his glasses up, "You never took me along just to translate Spanish for you."

"You don't speak Spanish," I said.

"Good point."

I knew that taking Kevin along could be a mistake. The kid was too eager to be useful, and we sure didn't need to involve him in a police investigation. On the other hand, I wanted to talk to the people at the agency informally, and Kevin did speak Spanish. I had Kevin's cell on speed dial and called him. It was just about the time when school was letting out, and I hoped he had his phone on.

"Hello?"

"Can you meet me in front of the school in fifteen minutes?" I asked.

"I have practice today," he said.

"You got trouble, too," I said. "They're setting a hearing date for your case. You tell me what's most important—your practice or keeping you out of jail?"

"I'll be in front of the school," he said.

The department has a bunch of kids working in their garage who love to soup up the undercover vehicles, and Paul and I took one of the cars that practically jump from a standing start to sixty miles an hour but look like they need to be pushed to get them out of a supermarket parking lot. We picked Kevin up in front of the school, and he was immediately impressed with all the gadgets under the dashboard.

"Where are we going?" he asked.

"To the agency you told me about," I said. "You're going along unofficially as our interpreter if we need one."

"Why are we going there?"

"Connecting the dots," I said. "Whenever I get a case with a lot of loose ends—and this case has as many loose ends as I've ever seen—I like to start connecting dots. What I'm hoping for is to get some kind of picture that makes sense. You understand what I mean?"

"My dad used to say that if you ask a thousand questions, you always get the truth," Kevin said. "You just have to figure out where it is."

"I like that," I said.

"And the next time we hear it, he's going to make believe he said it first," Paul said.

We found the address. It was in a down-and-out neighborhood that had once been a housing project. The actual number was a church on a side street. On the entrance to the basement, there was a fancy sign that read GREENVILLE SERVICES.

"Can I help you?" A middle-aged Hispanic man looked up from his newspaper.

Paul flashed his badge and said that he would like to ask a few questions.

"By all means," the man answered.

"What's the deal on this agency?" Paul asked, coming directly to the point.

"Have a seat," came the answer. "My name is Hernandes, and my aunt and I basically run the agency. There are a lot of people in this community from Mexico, Central America, and the Caribbean. You have to know this, of course. There was a police investigation a few years ago, if I remember correctly. Do you want coffee?"

I said no the same time that Paul said yes. Then he said no the same time that I said yes.

Mr. Hernandes pointed to a coffeepot and started making coffee as he spoke. His English was better than mine.

"We had the same concerns as the police," he said. "Were the people being exploited? Were they being abused? So we started this agency."

"And named it Greenville," Paul said.

"Not really. There was a pawn shop down the street that closed and left the sign behind. It looked good, so . . . "

"We're really interested in one particular worker who came through this agency," I said. "A woman named Dolores . . . Dolores . . ."

I realized I didn't have her last name and looked toward Kevin. The kid shrugged and I was feeling stupid.

"Where does she work?"

"For the McNamaras," Kevin said.

"Oh, Dolores Ponce." Mr. Hernandes shook his head affirmatively. "She's been working with the agency for over four years. Maybe longer than that. You want to see her pay record?"

"Yes," I said.

A dark, middle-aged woman came in, and Mr. Hernandes said something to her in Spanish. She went to the coffeepot, looking over her shoulder at me and Paul as Hernandes went to a bookcase and took out a set of black-and-white composition books.

Sitting at the desk, he looked through the books

until he found an index tab that he wanted and then pushed the book across to me.

"This is her pay record," he announced. "She makes three hundred sixty per week, and we make sure that she gets it."

"And what do you get paid for her services?" Paul asked.

"The agency gets four hundred dollars a week from Mr. McNamara," Hernandes answered. "So you see we get just ten percent. This is a community service, not a rip-off."

"And if I speak to Dolores, she'll verify this?" I asked.

"Absolutely."

"Can I take this book with me?" Paul asked.

"It's our only copy," Mr. Hernandes said. "And if another policeman comes, we need to have a record. But you can take it next door to the drugstore. For ten cents a page, they'll make copies."

Officially, we weren't investigating Greenville and we didn't have a search warrant. Hernandes seemed on the up and-up, but I wasn't sure. The record keeping wasn't first-rate, but it didn't jump out at me as being criminal, either. Some entries were in pen and some in pencil. Not very professional.

"Are you giving us your word that these records are accurate?" I asked Hernandes as Paul pored over the entries in the book.

He ducked his head slightly and shrugged. "I think they are," he said. "We're not here to make money, just to help the community. As far as I know, they're accurate."

"How come here, she seemed to make more money?" Paul asked.

Hernandes looked at the entries that Paul was pointing at and shrugged again. "I don't know," he said. "But I see that she was getting paid by Mr. McNamara and someone else. It was Christmastime. Maybe she wasn't working for him but he gave her a gift. I really don't know."

"Christmas?" Kevin perked up.

"You know something?" I asked.

"That's when Christy's mom was in the hospital," Kevin said.

I decided that Paul and I had already moved beyond our authorization by questioning Hernandes, so it didn't particularly bother me to have him go next door and copy the pages at the drugstore. I reimbursed him for the four dollars and ten cents he was charged and took the copies with me.

"Coffee is good for the soul, officer," Hernandes said when the woman brought it over.

I didn't like the coffee, but I thanked Mr. Hernandes anyway.

"That wasn't coffee," Paul said when we had got back into our vehicle. "That was coffee-flavored mud."

"It's called espresso," I said. "I love the flavor, but my stomach can't take it."

"So what are we going to do now?" Kevin asked.

Paul looked at his watch. "I'm off in thirty minutes," he said. "I promised the old lady I'd take her out to dinner tonight."

"Where you taking her?" I asked.

"The Italian restaurant on Fairmount."

"You messed up that bad?" I asked. "That place costs a fortune."

"What can I tell you?" Paul said.

We drove to Paul's house and let him out. Then I started toward Kevin's place. On the way I told him what Pellingrino had told me. I tried to explain it as casually as I could because I didn't want him to panic. It must have been too casual, because he didn't seem bothered at all.

"Kevin, do you remember why Mrs. McNamara was in the hospital?"

"No, sir."

"Christy never told you?"

"No, sir."

"If you called Christy now, would she tell you?"

"I don't think so."

"You're lying."

"You can't call me a liar," he said. There was anger in his voice.

"I can drive you down to the juvenile facility," I said. "Charge you with something stupid, like obstruction of justice."

Silence.

"Is that what happens to you on the soccer field, too?" I asked. "You start off playing a team game and then you're the lone eagle, figuring out ways you can win all by yourself?"

"I don't mean to do that," he said. "It's just that . . . can you stop the car for a minute?"

I eased the car over to the right lane and then to a stop outside a drugstore. Three characters leaning against the wall looked at the car; then one of them put the brown paper bag they had been passing around into a pocket and they all took off slowly down the street.

"They must know you're a cop," Kevin said.

"They think everybody is a cop," I said. "What did you have to say?"

"I know you're on my side," Kevin said. "Just the fact that the judge called you was good. Even your partner seems like a nice guy. I just wish I could do more to straighten things out."

"Do what you can do, Kevin," I said. "That's what we expect from decent young men. We don't expect miracles, just that people contribute what they can to make this a better planet to live on."

"Christy doesn't tell me all that much," Kevin said. "In a way I don't want to know it, and in another way, it's easier between us for me not to know everything about her mother."

"Her mother?"

"Her mother went to the hospital a week after Christmas and Christy was all upset," Kevin said. "I ran into her after school and I saw she had been crying. She was trying to be calm but her hands were shaking. I mean, *really* shaking."

"She say anything to the school about her situation?"

"To a *teacher*? No."

"And the night of the accident?"

"She just called me and asked me to meet her," Kevin said. "When we met, she asked me not to ask her any questions."

"Where did you meet her?"

"About a half mile from where we were stopped. She was just sitting in the car with the lights off."

"Had she driven the car to that spot?"

"Yeah. She wanted me to get in."

"Where were you two going?"

"I don't think we had a plan," Kevin said. "Not too smart, huh?"

"You remember the name of the hospital?"

"It was the one outside of Eatontown," he said.

"Monmouth? Monmouth Memorial?"

"Yeah, that's the one," Kevin said. "It's got a gift shop in the lobby."

We sat for a few moments more without speaking. Kevin put his head down on the dashboard and I pulled him back up. He might have known more, but it had taken a lot for him to open up the way he had.

"One of the best pieces of advice I ever had was from an old man who lived down the street from me when I was your age," I said. "He told me that when I meant to do well to give myself the benefit of the doubt. I'm giving that same advice to you."

I took Kevin home and called Carolyn from the car to tell her I was going to be late. She asked me if everything was all right with Kevin, and I told her that the picture was getting a little clearer.

Getting information from a hospital is tough business. You need to either be a relative or produce a court order. Either way they will tell you as little as they possibly can. I wanted to know why Mrs. McNamara had been admitted to the hospital, but I didn't want to do anything to get her husband in trouble. No matter how I looked at the situation, I had to remind myself that McNamara wasn't the one facing charges for being in the car that night; Kevin was.

I called on Monday morning, identified myself as a police officer, and inquired about Mrs. McNamara's admission. I was put on hold for a full three minutes before a woman came on and asked what I wanted. I repeated my request and she took down all the particulars about what precinct I worked in, my badge number, the whole nine yards.

"We really can't give any information except for the fact that she was brought to the emergency ward by the police in Red Bank."

"Was she injured? Hit by a car? What?"

"We can't give out that information without a court order, sir." She seemed pleased with herself. "We can say that she left our hospital on the fourth of January. That was a Thursday."

"Thanks, you've been very helpful."

I called Red Bank and got a desk sergeant who said there was no record of anyone taking a woman to the hospital that day. He explained that the week before Christmas had been very busy and the paperwork probably hadn't been done.

I gave up on the hospital.

Monday afternoon Kevin called and told me his mother had received notification that the hearing would be on the sixteenth and was freaking out.

"She wants to know if we need to have a lawyer present," he said. "We don't have a lot of money."

"You don't need a lot of preparation for this hearing, but I'll ask around and let you know," I said. "I called the hospital today, but I couldn't get any information about Mrs. McNamara."

"Did you ask them about her meds?" Kevin asked. His voice was subdued. "She gets them from the hospital pharmacy."

"You think I should ask Mr. McNamara about the meds?" I asked.

"He won't tell you," Kevin said. His voice was barely audible. "He's really strange. Christy says he hardly ever speaks to her lately except for things that don't make sense. I can't figure him out."

"Do you think we can figure him out together?" I asked.

For a while there was no answer. I imagined Kevin holding the phone, his mind working overtime, and maybe deciding to clam up again.

"You want me to come to your house now?" he asked.

CHAPTER

12

I dropped my bike on the lawn and ran up the front walk of 238 Terrence Road. It was raining so hard that I could barely make out the numbers on Sergeant Brown's house. I wiped my muddy feet on the doormat and rang the bell.

Mrs. Brown opened the door and signaled for me to come in. "This is the rainiest season we've had in years," she said, smiling at me. "You'd better come in before you catch pneumonia."

I took my shoes off at the welcome mat.

"One minute!" a familiar voice shouted from another room in the house.

I heard heavy footsteps, and there was Sergeant Brown standing in front of me. "Sit down, Kevin," he said as he gestured to the couch. Then he gave his wife a look that meant get out of here.

"I'll leave you two alone to talk."

"I brought you some cookies," I said, stretching out my hand to give Sergeant Brown the wet bag.

He smiled. "Thank you," he said as he eagerly opened up the bag.

"Jerry!" Mrs. Brown yelled as she was walking out the door. "You've already had dessert!"

He rolled his eyes. "I know, I know, just a few."

Sergeant Brown's house had a cozy feel to it. On the mantel, there were several pictures of him and his wife.

"Is that you?" I asked, pointing to a picture of a young-looking man wearing an army uniform.

"No, that's my son. He looks a lot like me."

"He's in the army?"

"Yes, he's a drill sergeant at a training camp in Texas,"

he replied. "So you wanted to talk, Kevin?" Sergeant Brown relaxed into a black leather armchair.

"You know, Sergeant Brown, I really shouldn't be in all this trouble. I didn't really carjack a car and do all the stuff that people said I did."

Sergeant Brown leaned toward me. "So what happened?"

I hesitated, knowing once I told him, there was no turning back.

"After soccer that night, I was just kind of daydreaming in my room when Christy called me. She sounded pretty upset and she asked me to meet her down at the park. I asked her what was going on, but she didn't want to tell me over the phone. I wasn't even sure that I wanted to go, but I did."

"You had a friend in trouble," Sergeant Brown said.

"Yes, and I like Christy; we've been friends since preschool. She's not stuck up and she doesn't act like a drama queen in school," I said. "She had spoken to me before about her problems. But after my dad died, I didn't feel I could help anyone with their problems, and we'd been growing apart. When Christy called, she swore me to secrecy. I said I would meet her. I grabbed a jacket and walked down to where she said she'd be. She wasn't there yet, so I sat down on a bench to wait for her."

"Then what happened?" Sergeant Brown asked, looking intently at me.

I hesitated. I was wishing that I hadn't come and hadn't started talking to Sergeant Brown.

"I thought she'd be walking from the direction of the entrance to the park, near Riverdale, and I was looking that way when a car screeched to a halt on the road near me. I was a little startled, but I didn't think much of it until the window rolled down and I saw Christy behind the wheel. I did a double take and went up to the car window. She told me to get in and I did.

"Christy was really upset. Her face was wet, and even in the darkness of the car, I could see that her hair was sticking to her cheeks. I knew she had been crying for a while. All kinds of things went through my mind. I thought maybe somebody had hurt her or something. I was already thinking about calling the police.

"'What's wrong?' I asked.

"Christy pulled herself together after a while and reached over and took my hand. Her hand was wet, and it sent a chill through me.

"'Do you remember when I told you about my mom

having problems?' she asked.

"I told her I did.

"'Things have gotten worse.' She told me that her dad had hit her mom. 'I can't stand it! I can't stand it anymore!' she said.

"I didn't know what to say, so I didn't say anything."

"There are times when saying nothing is the only good thing to say," Sergeant Brown said.

"Christy started telling me about her mother's depression, how she sometimes would start crying in the middle of a conversation, or would go and sit in the dark by herself. Her dad didn't know how to deal with it and would try to force her out of being depressed. He used to yell at her a lot, but now he was hitting her and pushing her around."

Mrs. Brown came into the room carrying two glasses of milk for us. I thanked her and Sergeant Brown smiled. Our conversation stopped until she left the room.

"Okay, it's making more sense now," Sergeant Brown said, resting his chin on his hand.

"Christy said she just couldn't take it anymore. The therapist had told them they would have to watch out for her mom so that she didn't kill herself, but sometimes—and

Sergeant Brown, this is what really freaked me out—Christy said that sometimes she felt that she wanted to kill herself, too. It made her feel so depressed to think about putting her mother in the hospital. 'Like some kind of animal or something.' That's how Christy put it.

"I didn't know what to do. Christy was talking about suicide. My stomach was turning something crazy. I mean, what do you think I should have said? 'I'm sorry you're going to kill yourself but I can't help you because I'll get in trouble'? I would much rather get arrested and go to juvie than have a friend kill herself!"

"Kevin, there were other ways to help her besides getting behind the wheel of a car. How did you think you were helping her by doing that?"

"She asked me to help her. I told her that we could call the hospital and see if someone there could help her mom. I told her we shouldn't drive the car back to her house. I offered to have my mom come and return the car, but Christy said no.

"'As soon as my father finds out that the car's gone,' Christy told me, 'I'm going to have to answer a thousand questions from him. He's starting to act as crazy as she is.'

"By this time, she was crying again. A lot. She didn't want to have to deal with her father, and I couldn't blame her—he's got such a bad temper. I guess I did something stupid. Maybe I shouldn't have helped her. I didn't know what else to do."

For the first time since I began talking, I relaxed a bit.

Sergeant Brown nodded. "And you decided to drive the car back to Christy's house?"

"She couldn't really drive very well. Christy made me. I've only driven around a parking lot in my cousin's car," I said, "but I wanted to get the car back to her house as much as Christy did. She was shaking so bad that when she asked me to drive, we switched places. I got behind the wheel. The park wasn't far from Christy's house, and I thought I could get there all right."

"And that's when you crashed the car and got arrested?"

"Everything was okay when I started driving," I said. "But then Christy's cell phone rang and I thought it was going to be her father. It was just a girl from school, but it made me distracted enough that I didn't look before I changed lanes. It wasn't a big accident, just a few dents, but when the other driver saw how young I was and Christy in the car, he jumped to a lot of conclusions. He backed away from the car and called the police. Before I knew it, I was in handcuffs."

"What did you tell the arresting officer?" Sergeant Brown asked.

"All the while we were waiting, Christy was saying that we couldn't tell the whole story about her dad hitting her mom, because then he would be arrested."

"Automatic domestic violence," Sergeant Brown said.

"And then everyone would know about her mom's depression, and maybe she would end up being put in the hospital," I said.

"That was one messed-up night, wasn't it?"

"What would you have done, sir?" I asked.

"Well, if I were my age and wore a badge, it wouldn't have been a problem." Sergeant Brown was actually chuckling to himself. "But if I were your age and didn't want to betray my friend, I would have sat there and stammered until they took me to juvenile."

"That's what I did," I said. "I thought if I just blabbed everything, the police would put her father in jail and her mother in an institution. And I don't want her to grow up without a father, Sergeant Brown. I know what that's like and . . . I wouldn't want it to happen to anyone. No matter what her father is like."

The room was so silent, I could hear the faint ticking of the clock.

"Don't you feel better now that you told someone, Kevin?" Sergeant Brown said.

"I do. I couldn't tell my mom or my *abuela* because they've been through so much. . . . I don't want to go back to juvie! I don't belong there. Do you think they'll send me back?" I asked, feeling nervous again.

Sergeant Brown looked thoughtful.

I went on. "I want to help Christy and her mom. Her mom *really* needs help, but both Christy and her dad are afraid that if they put her in the hospital, she won't get out."

"Kevin, I might, just might, have an idea that will help Christy's mom and keep you from going back to juvie. Let me think about this some more."

I gave a sigh. It felt good, like I was letting out all the bad feelings I'd had for weeks.

"It's late. Do you need a ride home, Kevin?" Sergeant Brown asked.

"Thanks, but I rode my bike and it looks like the rain

has stopped." I called good-bye to Mrs. Brown. At the door I shook Sergeant Brown's hand.

"Thanks for all your help, Sergeant Brown. I feel a lot better."

I walked to the lawn and straightened up my bike. No sooner had I started riding than I felt a drop of rain slide down my face. Then another and another, until it began to pour. I put the hood up on my sweatshirt and rode off fast, in sixth gear, then stopped pedaling as I went down a hill. It took me only a second to go all the way down the hill on my bike, but it seemed like it took months for me to climb back up. I guess life was a lot like that, too.

I couldn't see anything in front of me—only the headlights of cars coming up the hill. The rain was blowing into my face, and I stood up on the pedals. I stayed close to the curb. I thought of how stupid I was, biking like this in the rain. I should have taken Sergeant Brown up on his offer. Yet the raindrops hitting my skin felt cool and refreshing.

"C'mon, Ref!" parents whined.

"Hey, Ref, who's paying you?" one of our team's dads shouted.

Our team was losing by a goal midway through the first half of the semifinals at Fort Dix. And Nick, our goalie, was down after being kicked in the stomach trying to save a goal that the ref allowed.

"One more comment and you're out of here!" the ref yelled back.

The sidelines were overflowing with people: scouts, parents, friends, and players from other teams who wanted to watch us. My mom had taken the day off, and she was there with my grandma and Sergeant Brown.

As Coach Hill carried Nick to the sideline, parents from the opposing teams were shouting at one another on the sidelines. We didn't even have a backup goalie. Coach signaled one of our biggest kids, Matt, to take Nick's place. But we needed Matt defensively.

The other team, the New Jersey Arsenal Warriors, was a passing team that controlled the ball and barely let it get into our hands. As the game went on, I was growing less and less confident that we would win. I was exhausted and desperately needed water. I signaled with my hands for Coach to send in a sub for me, but he told me to tough it out. He had called a four-hour practice on Thursday night, and the whole team was beat and unfocused.

Ricky and I had no help up top, and we were just chasing the ball as the defenders played with it. I was regretting putting Under Armor on—sweat ran down my forehead and got into my eyes. It stung my eyes, since I had put sunblock on this morning.

The other team's best player was Lucas, their left midfielder, who was from Brazil. I figured I wouldn't run into him too often since I usually hung out on the other team's last defender. Cal shifted over to guard him. Cal was taller than Lucas, so I thought he wouldn't have any trouble winning the balls in the air. But I was wrong. This kid could jump higher than anyone I'd ever seen.

Matt swept up the shot and punted it out of the goal. It landed near Shawn, and he trapped it and brought it down to the ground softly.

"Right here!" I shouted. Shawn saw me from across the field and made a long pass that curved a little. It landed perfectly at my feet, and I ran down the edge of the field. Pressured by a defender, I knew I was one step ahead of him and my shot wouldn't get blocked. I crossed it with my left foot, and the ball landed right next to Ricky. Ricky received the ball near the goal. The goalie came out to get it, but Ricky knocked it away with his hip and then slid to tap the ball into the goal.

The crowd erupted into cheers. Coach Hill yelled, "Nice job, Ricky! Nice job with your left foot, Kevin!"

A few moments later the whistle blew, signaling half-time. Coach yelled at us to come over and sit.

"Thanks," Ricky said as we picked up our water bottles. I gave him a smile, and this time it wasn't sarcastic. I meant it. Something felt different for me in this game. I felt looser, less anxious—and maybe that was because I had gotten things off my chest by talking to Sergeant Brown. Who would have thought that would help my game? Soccer was the only thing on my mind.

"You guys are lucky to be tied," Coach Hill said as we sat down on the sidelines. "They're outplaying you guys, and they had just one quick lapse on defense. You've come a long way since the beginning of the season, and you should be proud of yourselves, whether you win or lose this game. But you're still not looking like the team I know you are. To win, you're going to have to show more teamwork, like Shawn and Ricky and Kevin just showed." Coach paused. "Now tell me, guys, are you having fun?"

"Yeah, Coach," we mumbled.

"It sure doesn't sound like it. Look, I know I've been tough on you the past couple of weeks, but that's only because I want you to succeed. Now I don't expect you to be perfect, and I know you think I do, but I don't. Perfection only drives people to achieve great things, but is never achieved. I'm just hard on you because I want you to try your best and give it your all, and if that's what you do, I'll be satisfied and you'll be satisfied, whatever the outcome."

It sounded like Coach knew that this would likely be the end of our season, and it was his way of saying good-bye. I had never seen this side of Coach Hill. Maybe he was seeing another side of me, too.

"So go out and enjoy this moment, because who knows when it might come again," Coach added. We put our hands in. "One, two three, Raiders!" we shouted.

We came out in the second half with renewed energy and disrupted their style of play by playing man-to-man. The minute they passed the ball, one of our players would close them down and force a turnover. The momentum was changing.

At the end of the second half, the score was still 1–1. Since it was a State Cup game, we had to go into a fifteen-minute overtime. At the end of that, if there was no winner, it would go into another fifteen-minute overtime. Penalty kicks were the last option. They put a lot of pressure on the goalies and the kickers.

The Arsenal Warriors started with the ball. Ty was fouled just outside the eighteen-yard box. Coach ordered Cal to take it, since he had the best foot. Cal moved the ball a little bit up when the ref wasn't looking, and the Warriors created a wall to try to block his view of the goal. Our team lined up to try to get the ball if there was a rebound.

This was the first time I'd ever seen Cal look nervous. He was usually pretty cool. He took the kick and put so much spin on it, it looked like it was in slow motion as it rotated. It hit the ground right underneath the goalie's spread-out arms and then bounced into the goal.

The crowd broke into cheers and our bench stood up in excitement.

But the danger was not over yet, as we still had to finish out the overtime. There were a few scary moments, but we managed to hold the other team off by keeping possession of the ball. By the end of the game, the Warriors were too frustrated and gave up on themselves. Their coach screamed at them to not give up and run after every ball, but I think they tuned him out.

We lined up and shook the hands of the opposing players. Their heads were down.

I wasn't sure that the better team had won, but I was overjoyed at the opportunity we now had.

I put my arm around Shawn, who had taken his shirt off in the celebration. "I didn't think we could do it," I said.

"Man, I know it's just the semis, but it feels like we won it all," Shawn yelled.

Coach Hill gathered us together. Looking over his shoulder, I saw the next semifinal game was getting ready to be played. We were more focused on that than on what Coach Hill was saying. But Coach was so happy with the win that he let it go.

The New Jersey Golden Eagles were one of the top teams in the country. They had won the past three State Cups and two regional titles. They came in second in the nation last year. It would take a miracle to beat them. You'd have to pull off some kind of stunning upset, the kind that would show up on the ESPN highlights in the morning—if ESPN cared about soccer.

I was psyching myself out for the finals. I didn't want to set the bar low, but I knew I would be cool with a silver medal.

After Coach's talk, he wanted us to go view the next game and learn about the opponent. I grabbed a sweatshirt from my soccer bag. Now that the game was over, I was freezing.

By the time we reached the sideline, the Golden Eagles were already up 1–0. This is going to be a blowout, I thought. The other team's offense looked lost. The Golden Eagles' best player was a black dude they called Kwame. Every time I saw the guy in a game, it was as if his whole life depended on every play.

"Not to be negative here, guys" I said, "but the only thing that our team is learning is that we're going to lose."

"Badly," Matt added. "Their team is full of stars."

"Look, guys, everyone is assuming that the Eagles are going to win," Shawn said. "But the truth is we don't have anything to lose if we give it all we got, and maybe we can just pull this thing off."

I didn't know if I was wrong to think that we were going to lose or whether I was just trying to be realistic. We'd find out in a week's time.

On the way home I thought of what Shawn had said and how the whole team felt about playing next week. There was a good chance we'd get our butts kicked, but if we didn't at least try, we were definitely going to lose.

I thought maybe I had been guessing all along that I had to lose in court, too. I still figured I was going to be toast, but I did have a play in the back of my head. I went straight to my room. I found the number I was looking for on speed dial and pressed the button.

"Hello, Sergeant Brown, could I talk to you about Christy and her dad?"

CHAPTER
13

"Jerry, do you know what you're getting into with this dinner?" Carolyn asked.

"Nope."

"Then why are we going?"

"Because it's a chance to maneuver McNamara into a place where he might feel like being a good guy."

"Why don't you just sit him down and tell him how nice that boy is?" Carolyn had slipped on her serious face. "Tell him that Kevin isn't a thief."

"If McNamara had been in the mood to listen to the world, we wouldn't be dealing with him, woman," I said.

"And if those kids had any common sense . . ." Carolyn's lips tightened slightly.

"Look, those kids were stuck between a rock and a hard place. Christy is smart enough to know her mother needs some kind of professional help, and she's clever enough to understand that what her father's doing— trying to control his wife's behavior and to bully her into good behavior—isn't going to work. That night he was pushing his wife—Christy's mother—around, and the girl just couldn't take it anymore. That started the whole chain of events."

"She should have called—somebody!" Carolyn said.

"Like who?" I asked. We were attending a dinner and get-together at Kevin's house that I hoped would begin to ease things up a bit.

"I don't know their family," my wife answered.

"We've had problems in the past and we didn't reach for a phone," I said. "We hung on to those problems, trying to keep them within our household until something came along to solve them. What do you expect from people as young as Kevin and Christy?"

"But getting into a car . . . " Carolyn didn't finish her sentence.

I knew what she meant, but I'd also had enough experience over the years dealing with people who had problems to know that the simple answers were always easy when they were somebody else's problems.

"I've seen parents tell their children to lie to the police because it seemed to them the only way out of a difficult situation," I said. "And sometimes I thought they were right."

"Would you lie to get out of trouble?" Carolyn looked at me, and I glanced at her.

"To hold my family together?" I asked. "To protect you? Yeah, I would lie. If I couldn't think of anything else. The girl was trying to hold her family together, and she didn't want her father to get into trouble."

"Lord, lord, lord." Carolyn shook her head.

"Look, everybody knows what's going on and everybody's a little scared," I said. "The thing is that there just aren't any easy answers."

"That's why he's coming to this dinner?"

"No, like I told you, Kevin asked me to invite the McNamaras to dinner. He asked me if I would come.

You're coming along to show everybody that it's just a friendly dinner."

"And why is McNamara coming along?"

"One thing I've learned from my years on the force is that people act because they've either made a decision or they're close to making a decision," I said. "McNamara wants to know how hostile we'll be to him or his situation and if we're really on his side. What he senses tonight will push him one way or the other. That's why he said he'd come to this dinner. Now, can we get going?"

"And you're sure of this?"

"Nope."

"But you're convinced that this dinner is going to work?"

"Nope. But I got my fingers crossed and a song in my heart," I said.

"You're as bad as Kevin!"

"Or as good—if it works," I said.

"Hope that song doesn't end up on a blues note," Carolyn said. "What does Mrs McNamara do that's odd, anyway?"

"Sounds like depression to me," I said. "I looked up the symptoms on the internet."

"Jerry, that is the worst thing you could have done. You're not supposed to be looking up people's symptoms on the internet and making judgments about them. What did it say?"

"It said that depression was serious and you had to be careful with it," I said.

"It say anything about chicken soup?"

"Kevin thinks that we shouldn't work on Mrs. McNamara," I said. "He thinks we should work on Mr. McNamara. He thinks that if Mr. McNamara sees everybody is friendly, he'll come around."

"He won't," Carolyn said.

"You don't know that," I said.

I fixed the rearview mirror and drove the rest of the way to Kevin's house in silence. Carolyn was right. McNamara hadn't been friendly at all when I spoke to him on the phone, but he had asked some interesting questions. The most interesting was whether Kevin had "talked a lot of guff" about what had happened that night. I thought what he wanted to know was if anybody was thinking of charging him with domestic violence against his wife. That would have revealed his whole situation and opened a can of worms that maybe should have been open, but that McNamara wasn't ready to deal with.

"And why does Kevin think he's even going to show up?" Carolyn asked.

"Because Kevin is as good a young man as we think he is," I said. "And like most kids his age, he believes everyone else in the world is just *waiting* for the chance to do the right thing. And you know what? I like that attitude. I really do."

"But he did say he was coming," Carolyn said. "So I guess he'll at least show."

I remembered the phone conversation. The strain in McNamara's voice told me he had some serious reservations about the dinner.

My mind kept switching to the car. I imagined I heard something wrong with the engine, and then the lights seemed dimmer than usual. By the time we reached Kevin's place, it was my stomach that needed the tune-up.

"Look, Carolyn, anything you can do to help tonight will be appreciated," I said.

"Jerry, I've been putting up with you for almost thirty-nine years," she answered. "I kind of get the routine by now. We go in, it gets messed up, and then all the way home you tell me how right I was. Isn't that how it works?"

Kevin's house was all lit up with candles. There were real candles on the mantelpiece and on the end tables. Others, placed around the room, were electric. They gave the place a warm glow but enough dark shadows to add drama. Kevin's grandmother gave me a big hug and then kissed Carolyn. She turned and said something to her daughter in Spanish.

"She's saying your wife has the same color as cinnamon," Kevin said.

"I used to think of her as brown sugar," I said. "I guess cinnamon fits her now."

Estela, Kevin's mother, took Carolyn into the kitchen, and the grandmother stood in front of me with a big smile on her face. I didn't know what to say, so I just smiled back. Finally she patted me on the shoulder and went to join Estela.

"Sometimes she speaks great English," Kevin says. "But when she tries to get fancy, she has to speak Spanish in her mind and then she can't find the words in English. Then she just looks at you."

"I can understand that," I said. "It happens to me

when I want to sound super-intelligent. Have you heard from you-know-who?"

"Christy's been working on her mother, trying to get her excited about coming," Kevin said. "She told her that she wants to learn how to cook Colombian food."

"You kids ought to be politicians," I said. "You spend your life scheming away."

The women returned with plates of cheese and crackers, something that looked like peas in cream, some midget bananas, and sodas. I liked the way Carolyn was mixing in. If she had a good time, the trip home wouldn't be so bad.

Kevin put on some music and we sat around and talked. Somehow, the conversation got to be about the differences between dogs in the United States and dogs in Colombia.

"In my country, *un perro es un perro*." Kevin's grandmother hit the middle of her left palm with her right index finger for emphasis. "In this country, *un perro es un* kink!"

"A king," Kevin said.

"It's what I said," his grandmother went on. "*Un* kink! They have more food for dogs in the market than for *bebés*!"

I couldn't argue with that, and it was a good assessment of American values. People loved their dogs and were willing to pamper them.

Carolyn and I had arrived on time for dinner at six thirty. There was no sign of the McNamara family. When the clock on the wall had reached seven thirty, Mrs. Johnson finally suggested we sit down and eat. I glanced at Kevin and he shrugged, clearly disappointed. I felt disappointed too, and frustrated.

"I had hoped that Mr. McNamara would come," I said to Estela. "I was surprised that he said he would, but I knew it was a long shot."

Kevin's mother forced a smile and nodded. Then she gestured to the table. Life moved on.

We sat down and the grandmother had just placed a tureen of soup in the middle of the table when the doorbell rang. I caught my breath, and for a long moment we all froze around the table. Then Kevin's mom wiped her hands on the front of her dress and went to answer the door.

The suit McNamara wore, a light brown double breasted with patch pockets, looked at least a size too large for him. The shirt he wore looked clean but not crisp. I knew he was uncomfortable as he shifted from foot to foot during the introductions. We sat with me, Carolyn, and Kevin's grandmother on one side of the table, the McNamaras at the other side, and Kevin and his mother at either end.

Christy's mom, close up, was an attractive woman. She had wispy brown hair just long enough to touch the bottom of her jawline. Her face was thin, youthful looking, with a touch of makeup. I imagined Christy making her mother up.

But it was her hands that I noticed most. It was as if there was no place for them. She put them on the table, then on her lap, then folded and unfolded them inches from the table. She had smiled nervously at everyone as she was being introduced, making sure not to make too much eye contact.

"It's avocado soup," Kevin's mom said. "Kevin loves anything with avocados in it."

"He's a dreamer," his grandmother said, rubbing his head in a way that I knew he didn't want Christy to see. "Everything is too much, like Florentino Ariza in . . . I don't remember the book. But he falls in love with every star and every moon he sees. Isn't that right, Kevin?"

"Abuela!" Kevin shook his head. "I don't fall in . . . "

"I like romantic boys," Carolyn said. "I used to go out with a boy who used to tell me that my teeth were like pearls and my eyes were like precious jewels. He owned a pawn shop when he grew up."

I glanced over at Christy's father. He was staring down at his plate, and I was sure he was thinking the whole idea of coming to the dinner had been a mistake.

"When Kevin's father was really young . . . " Kevin's mom sat down at the table and in a minute, Kevin's mom, Carolyn, and his grandmother were deep into a discussion about boys they had known when they were young. Christy's mom sat shoulders slumped, wringing her hands in her lap.

McNamara was sitting next to his wife and keeping a close eye on her. I saw his jaw tightening and relaxing, as if he were trying hard to control himself. Christy was eating the avocado soup, clearly tense, watching her mother.

I tried to think of something to say to Mr. McNamara, but everything I thought of sounded stupid even before I opened my mouth. I wanted to sneak a peek at the clock. I started doing the math. Fifteen minutes for the soup. Thirty minutes for the main course. Twenty minutes for dessert. Twenty minutes for polite conversation, and then two hours of Carolyn's mouth before I got to sleep.

"Do you like avocados?"

Silence.

I looked up and saw that Kevin's grandmother was talking to Mrs. McNamara.

"Do you like avocados?" she asked again.

"She doesn't like soup very much," Mr. McNamara interjected.

"*Love in the Time of Cholera.*" Mrs. McNamara lifted her head. "That was the name of the book. *Love in the Time of Cholera.*"

"That was it!" Kevin's grandmother's face lit up. "Did you read that book? I have it in Spanish. That man, Florentino, I could have married. Of course, I wouldn't have married him, but I could have. You know what I mean?"

"I do. He was a wonderful character," Mrs. McNamara said.

And then the conversation was between Kevin's grandmother and Mrs. McNamara at one end of the table and Carolyn and Kevin's mother on the other end.

"You do the math?" Kevin was talking to Christy.

She shook her head no.

Okay, everybody was talking except me and McNamara.

I decided to take a chance.

"You want to grab some air?" I asked, standing.

He hesitated, and for a moment I thought I had lost him. I gave him a nod and started toward the door. He came.

Somebody in the neighborhood had cut their grass that afternoon, and the smell was sweet in the warm summer air. In the distance, a half-moon hung like it was painted over the houses.

"You know, there's help for people who have problems with their nerves," I said. "A captain from the force— real good guy—went over to that medical center off the service road that leads to the mall. They helped him a lot when he was dealing with a bout of depression."

"You're all up in my business, ain't you?" McNamara came back.

"You think that's because of all the years I've had as a cop?" I asked. "Maybe I got the habit?"

He patted his pockets, then shook his head. "I keep forgetting I'm supposed to be giving up smoking."

"That's good," I said, trying to think of something else to say.

"Yeah, I guess," McNamara said. We turned and went back inside Kevin's house.

I tried again to come up with something to say and couldn't. He didn't say anything, either, and I hoped he was feeling as stupid as I was.

The food wasn't bad. It just seemed to me not to be real food. A little too exotic, maybe. Or a little too spicy. Or just strange, like the capers in cream. Anyway, we survived the dinner. We were having little cakes that were too sweet and wine, which was even sweeter, when McNamara said he had to leave.

"Long day," he grunted.

"You have to come again." Kevin's grandmother patted Mrs. McNamara's wrist.

Mrs. McNamara smiled; she looked over at her husband, and quickly down.

Mr. McNamara shook hands with Kevin's people and me as quickly as he could and left with his arm around his wife's shoulder. I followed them out onto the porch and patted Mr. McNamara's arm. He turned, and I realized he was slightly taller than I had thought.

"This is my first real Spanish meal," I said quietly. "I'll have to decide if I like it."

"It was okay," he said. "I liked it."

"Look, if you want to talk to me anytime . . ."

"Because of the kids?" he asked, nodding toward where Kevin and Christy stood.

"Yeah, because of the kids," I said. "And because I'm an easy guy to talk to."

I watched the McNamaras as they walked away, looking for clues to how things had gone, but there weren't many. I liked his referring to Kevin and his daughter as "the kids," but I didn't want to read too much into it.

Carolyn and I stayed for a while longer before leaving, but not without a plate full of Colombian goodies to eat later.

"So, how did you like the food?" Carolyn asked as we reached the short stretch of highway on the way home.

"Good," I said.

"You ate enough of it," she said. "That's probably why they gave you that plate to take home. I'll bet they're still talking about how you gobbled up that chicken."

"Carolyn, I did not gobble up the chicken," I said. "It's only polite to eat what you're given."

"And when she asked you if you wanted some more, you said yes, and she piled your plate up and you downed that like there was no tomorrow," my wife went on.

"So what did you think of Christy's mother?" I asked.

"She's a little nervous," Carolyn said. "I thought I saw her almost lose it once, but she hung in there. Somebody—I think it was Kevin's mother was talking about how warm it was for this time of year, and Mrs. McNamara got a little teary. I think that sometimes women want that kind of light conversation. Sometimes we miss it."

We got home and turned on the late news. Same things on the news as the day before. Some teenaged pop singer was arrested for drunk driving, there was a stickup in the mall and the robber had shot himself trying to conceal the weapon from the closed-circuit cameras, and a professor in Australia was warning about the coming of a new Ice Age. And my stomach was beginning to hurt.

"Woman, where did you put the antacid tablets?" I asked.

"Your stomach bothering you?"

"No, I want to put them in my ears!" I said. "Why do you want to ask me a foolish question like that?"

"You shouldn't have eaten so much," Carolyn said. The Grand Inquisitor at work. "That was South American food and you have an African-American belly. All that rumbling I hear is your stomach trying to translate what it's got in it."

I listened to her mouth for another fifteen minutes, trying to pretend I was asleep so she would shut up, but whenever she stopped yapping, my stomach started growling again. Then the phone rang.

"Sergeant Brown?"

"Yes?"

"Yeah, this is Mike McNamara. Look, that place you were talking about down at the medical center? Is it open tomorrow?"

"It's open," I said. "You want the number?"

McNamara said yes, and my hands were shaking as I scrolled through my BlackBerry to find it. I gave it to him. He read it back carefully, told me he would give them a call, and mumbled a nearly inaudible "Thanks."

"You okay, man?"

"The world is still spinning, I guess," he said. "I don't know, I'll give them a call."

"Who was that?" Carolyn asked when I had hung up.

"McNamara," I said. "He said he was going to call the mental health clinic."

"Look at you, getting all emotional," Carolyn said.

My stomach was aching, but I felt great. I checked the time and saw that it was far too late to call Kevin.

Anyway, Christy would probably tell him the good news when he saw her in school.

"The world is still spinning." I had heard the expression before. I was questioning a prisoner, a young man who had been sentenced to twenty-five years to life and had asked him how he was doing. He had said that the world was still spinning and that nobody was caring how he felt or what he was thinking.

"It's spinning and people were going on with their lives while I just sit here," he said.

McNamara had seen a part of the world spinning, had sat down with Kevin's family and me and Carolyn and watched the world spin in a good and gentle way, and had decided it was time for him to join us. God, I felt good.

CHAPTER
14

The sound of my alarm clock made me shuffle across the room to turn it off. I couldn't put my alarm clock right by my bed because I would just press the snooze button every morning and end up being an hour late to school.

As I ate the breakfast that Abuela had made, I thought about the big game today. I'd gotten up early because it always takes me so long to get myself ready for major things. There are a whole bunch of minor things that need to get done to make the major things happen. You might have a major thing scheduled every day, or even once a week, but you can't just walk into one unprepared. You gotta get yourself ready, and that's what takes me so long—getting the minor things done.

I tried to keep my mind off the dinner last night, but I thought it went pretty well. It was hard to tell.

The phone rang on the kitchen counter and I reached over my plate of scrambled eggs and toast to get it.

"Hey, this is Christy. May I speak to Kevin?" she said.

"You're talking to him," I answered.

"I was wondering if you wanted to go to the park for a little while before your big game," she said, sounding happy.

"Yeah, it's at four, so I think I'll have time. I have to leave for the game at one thirty."

"I have some good news. My dad talked to Sergeant Brown last night and said that he wasn't going to press any charges."

I was so happy, I didn't know what to say. "Really? That's great."

"I thought you'd like to hear that. You want to meet

around like one o clock?"

"I'll be there," I said. "Wait a minute, Christy, you won't be driving there, right?"

"Nope." She laughed.

"Promise?"

"Promise."

My mom and grandma were unbelievably happy when I told them I wasn't going back to juvie. I was, too. I had a clean slate, and I wasn't going mess it up this time. Everything had happened so fast, but I sensed that my life was about to return to normal.

When I got to the bench, it was empty and I took a seat. Everything felt like it had before I had gotten myself into trouble. A car like the one Christy had driven that evening passed by, making me jump for a moment, until I realized of course it wasn't her.

"Hey, Kevin."

I turned around to see Christy smiling.

"You scared me," I said.

"Ha, I didn't mean to."

"What'd you want to meet about?" I asked.

"I wanted to tell you my dad agreed to let my mom get help at the hospital. I think that's really going to make her better this time."

"That's great!" I said. "Sergeant Brown is a good guy—I guess he knew how to make things right." I looked up at Christy. "I think I'd still be in jail if I hadn't met him."

Christy smiled again.

"And I'm *really* happy your dad decided to drop the charges," I added, smiling.

"Me, too, especially since the whole thing was *my* fault."

I was glad she knew that.

Everything was getting better. But there was one more important thing I still had to take care of. "If your mom's gonna be getting help, is Dolores still gonna be working at your house?" I asked her.

"Yeah, she just started working for a new agency. My dad has to pay more now, but she's so good with my mom. We really need her."

Yes! Sergeant Brown must have come through—once again.

"Oh that's really good, I like Dolores. She reminds me a little of my mom."

"Yeah, she's been with us for a long time. She's like part of the family."

We sat and talked a little more, and then my mom pulled up in her car, with my grandma in the front seat.

"Good luck at your game, Kevin."

I said good-bye to Christy and I got in. I was happy to hear Christy's good news, but I had to get focused. I would have time to think about it after we won our game.

I tried to sleep on the way to Fort Dix, but my nerves kept me awake. There's no glory for the team that comes in second, I thought. I could name most of the World Cup champions and which year they won, and I knew most of the NBA champions and Super Bowl champions over the past decade. But no one knew the teams they played against, the teams that came in second. It would make me sick to have an amazing season but to end up second best. No one would remember you. I knew I shouldn't be thinking our team was going to lose.

I might get only one chance in my whole entire life to be here, I thought, so I don't want to have any regrets, like I could have gotten to that ball and scored, and I could have made that penalty kick.

Coach saw that our team was tired and gave us a look.

"You guys get good sleep last night like I told you?" he asked.

"Yeah." The team yawned.

It was the beginning of November, and it was cold and windy. The shots would probably be all over the place.

I watched the Golden Eagles run perfectly executed drills in their gold-and-white uniforms.

But I wasn't going to be intimidated.

Coach had us do some light jogging to warm up and wake us up.

Sergeant Brown arrived before the game started. Mrs. Brown was with him, too. They were sitting next to my mom and Abuela.

Mom and my grandma had made a big deal about me being in the finals. I had heard Mom talking on the phone with my cousin Carolina in Colombia. She was saying how proud she was that I was in it.

After our warm-up, Coach called us in for the lineup and our team huddled together.

"Today is going to be a day for fun, but also lots of hard work. You've accomplished so much to get here. I hope you guys will enjoy yourselves out there, because

185

I know I certainly will. I know you guys are anxious, and probably nervous, too, but I want you to walk away from the field today and have no regrets. I don't want us to say, well, we had a bad game, we just didn't give it our all. I want you guys to leave it all out on the field. And if you do that, no matter what the score is, you'll walk away feeling good about yourselves."

The Golden Eagles started with the ball and kept it. They looked like they were in no rush by passing back and forth, being patient. Our defense was good because we weren't letting them get any good looks at the goal, but it was also too tentative, so we weren't able to get possession of the ball.

We were trying to double-team Kwame, their star forward. To be honest, I was sort of starstruck by him and in awe of his skills. Kwame looked at ease, like he was born to play soccer.

He used his speed to cut through ahead of our defenders as they played him a long ball over everyone's heads. Once he caught up to the ball, he cut the ball with the outside of his foot, causing our defenders to lose momentum and their balance. Kwame then ran full speed at the next defender, put his body between the ball and the defender, and spun it. I heard some oohs and aahs from the crowd, and just as Cal finally made the tackle, Kwame released the ball when he had already fallen halfway down. It went into the upper left-hand corner of the goal, and Nick didn't have a prayer.

Kwame pointed to the number 35 on his jersey and pounded his chest.

A few moments later Kwame crossed another ball to their number 13, who headed into the goal, uncontested.

I started to go into a trance on the field; I was just watching the ball, not moving. I wasn't fatigued; it was more like this whole experience was mentally wearing me out. I made a couple of good passes and started to gain momentum, but the halftime whistle blew and stopped me. The score was Golden Eagles 2, Highland Raiders 0.

Coach Hill's tone was sharp. "I'm going to be frank with you guys now. I'm not happy with you—not happy at all. At the beginning I told you that I would be pleased regardless of the outcome as long as you were trying hard. Well, you're not. Be honest—how many of you guys expected to lose coming into this game?"

I looked around. Not one kid raised his hand. I slowly lifted my hand, until it was barely above my head. After that a few other hands came up, until slowly, one by one, almost every hand was up in the air.

"Well, there you go. How can you win a game that you expect to lose? It's that simple. I know most of you were probably thinking, Oh, we'll try and keep the score respectable, but if we let up one goal, we're finished. You're not trying hard. I don't care if this team is more talented than you as long as you show more heart. It's all about what's in here," he said, pointing to his own heart. "That's how it is in life. Someone can be better than you at something, but if you work hard, that's all that matters.

"Let me tell you something, I would rather have someone who works extremely hard, who is an all right player, than the best player in the world who is lazy. You guys need to fight for every ball and knock the opposing players down. Show them you're not afraid, and instead of trying to beat them at their game, beat them with yours."

I remembered one of my old coaches telling me that 2–0 was the most dangerous score in the game for the team that was up. If the team down scored once, then they would gain momentum, and the other team would, in a state of shock, give up another goal. Then the score would be tied. Maybe there was hope for us.

The game resumed and we were still trailing five minutes through, as expected. Number 4 on their team was becoming physical with me. We were nudging each other until it finally grew into a full-blown shove. On the corner kick, he turned his head to make sure the ref wasn't looking and blatantly pushed me. I raised my hand, about to give him what he deserved, but stopped. It just wasn't worth it.

I stood outside, about eighteen yards from the goal, ready to receive the corner kick that Cal was about to take. Learning how to receive a corner kick took a lot of skill; there needed to be a perfect balance of timing and jumping. I jumped and the ball coincidentally hit my head. I felt a body go up against the back of mine and the force sent me tumbling to the ground. I heard the sharp tone of the ref's whistle, and his hand shot out and pointed to the penalty box.

"Way to draw the penalty, Kevin!" Ricky exclaimed as he gave me a high five.

Coach told Cal to take it. I wasn't upset. I knew that for the sake of the team, and this game, Cal would be better off taking it than me.

Cal looked nervous—he was twirling a strand of his long light blond hair. He had done this with his hair a bunch of times before, in situations when he was either in trouble at school or under pressure.

Defending penalties is hard, and the goalies are always under extreme pressure. I expected the penalty to happen in slow motion, but as soon as the ref blew his whistle, Cal took it. It soared into the bottom right-hand corner.

We lifted up our heads. Maybe Coach was right about us needing to believe in ourselves.

The Golden Eagles didn't look worried, and that scared me. There was a confidence to them, a winning attitude.

Despite Cal's goal, I was running out of stamina. I started to slow down, but then I had a couple of nice crosses and passes. I was in the zone. A few plays later I received the ball from midfield, and there was no turning back. I ran past one defender, putting my body between the ball and him. Then I pushed off his body and used it as leverage to whip past him. Without thinking, I released the ball from outside the eighteen-yard line. It was a fast power shot that landed straight in the top right corner of the net. The goalie didn't have a chance.

The crowd erupted into cheers. I had even surprised myself. It was a once-in-every-hundred goals sort of shot.

We were tied with the second-best team in the nation. I was still in awe when my teammates ran over and high-fived me and put their arms around my shoulder.

The ref blew his whistle five minutes later, signifying the end of regulation time. I was surprised at how quickly the game had gone and how clutch my kick had been.

Coach Hill gave me a high five when I walked over to the sideline. "Now it's overtime. Let's get down to business."

Two gut-wrenching periods of overtime passed by, with the Eagles hitting the crossbar of our goal and with Ricky blowing a breakaway chance for us.

We were down to penalty kicks to break the tie.

"Guys, I'm going to give you the lineup for taking penalty kicks. First is Ricky, second Cal, third Matt, fourth Shawn, and kicking fifth Kevin."

Kicking fifth was the most pressured spot in the lineup, if the penalty kicks went that far. I remembered in the 2006 World Cup, it came down to the last kicker.

Both teams gathered at the halfway line. We put our arms around our teammates.

I stood with the four other kickers. It was all coming to an end, right here. Whichever team had made more shots at the end of their five kicks would be the winner.

Their first player, Kwame, easily made it. Ricky made it, too. Nick caught the next kick from the Golden Eagles, except the ball slipped through his hands. Every time a player went up to kick, both teams sucked in a big gulp of air and held their breath. Every time the ball went into the back of the net, you could hear a million sighs, and everyone's shoulders slumped down.

It was a shock when Calvin's ball went low and wide right, missing the goalpost by mere centimeters. He put his hands on his head in disbelief. It was all up to Nick now. He had to save one of the next three shots. The Eagles and our next two kickers made their penalties, leaving them up 4–3. If Nick didn't save this, I didn't even need to kick.

The Eagles' number 7 placed the ball on the penalty spot. He looked sort of nonchalant and cool as he put it on the line. I closed my eyes and flinched as I heard his foot hit the ball, but jumped up when I heard the ball bang against something. It was Nick's body! He had dived and saved it.

My feeling of happiness turned to anxiety as I realized the game rested on my shoulders. If I made it, we would need to go to a sudden-death round, where one kid from each team would kick until one kid missed and the other made it. If I missed, well, I didn't even want to think about that.

Their goalie was tall compared to Nick. It looked like he was trying to intimidate me by giving me a death stare.

Low left-hand corner, son, I heard my dad's voice in my head.

I took a deep breath and tried not to telegraph my pass. I put my whole body, mind, and everything I had into the shot.

Cling! The ball struck the outside of the post and bounced off.

We had lost. It was over.

It took a moment for me to take it all in. My teammates had their hands on their heads. But then a couple of them came over and put their arms around me. Eventually the field filled with family members and players.

"Hey, Thirteen," a deep voice called. I turned. It was Kwame.

"You played well, man. That was a tough break with the post. Maybe we'll meet again next year," he said, smiling.

That meant a lot to me.

"Thanks, man" was all I could manage to say.

I felt an arm around me and turned to see Sergeant Brown with my mom and Abuela. I was going to be okay.

On Sunday afternoon, Sergeant Brown called.

"Hey, Kevin," Sergeant Brown said. "How would you like to go to the Highland Middle School field and play some soccer? I've been working on my game."

"Meet you in a few minutes." I closed the front door and walked out with my best soccer ball in hand.

After our disappointing loss yesterday, I didn't feel like doing much of anything, but maybe going to play with Sergeant Brown would cheer me up.

I kept replaying that penalty kick in my mind, wishing I could have made it and had a chance to hold that trophy. But after I woke up this morning, I knew it was no good to think of it anymore and tried to force it out of my mind. It wasn't all bad, though. My life ended up a whole lot better than it was a few weeks earlier.

The trees outside had turned a Thanksgiving color. The leaves that fell littered the ground in wet clumps after last night's rain.

When I arrived, Sergeant Brown was sitting on a park bench.

"How are you feeling?" he asked me.

"Pretty down. But I guess it's not the end of the world. Especially after the way things started out with me in September."

"I'm glad you can see that. When I was a senior in high school, my team went to the city championships in basketball. I was fouled with four seconds left on the clock. All I needed to do was make one of two shots and the game would be sent to overtime. And do you know what happened?"

"What?"

"I missed them both. Yeah, it hurt for a while, but it didn't change who I was. Most people have stories like that, Kevin—it's just a part of life. You can't push your worries and bad feelings out to the side, because when you do that, you're giving them a chance to grow and weigh you down. You have to move on."

Hearing Sergeant Brown say that made me feel a lot better.

"Maybe now you'll think before you do stupid things."

Doing stupid things. That reminded me of something. "Sergeant Brown, I have a question to ask you. Whatever happened to the agency that was taking advantage of those immigrants? Christy said that they stopped using them and now Dolores is with a new agency that's paying her more."

"I called Mr. McNamara and persuaded him to fully cooperate in the investigation. Now that he knows me, I think he trusts me more. He even gave papers and pay records that can help us press charges."

"So you got them?"

"Yeah, and we needed someone like Mr. McNamara to come forward. All the illegal immigrants were afraid of being deported."

"So my detective work didn't really help?"

"Kevin, the address that you gave us helped, even though you didn't go about the right way of getting it. I told you, you'd make a good police officer someday."

I looked up at him.

"Well, I guess you're all straightened out now, aren't

you? You don't need me hanging around anymore, bugging you."

I was startled. My stomach fell as he stood up and kicked the ball. It missed my feet by a mile, and I went chasing after it.

A tall man playing baseball with his son smiled and then kicked the ball back.

"I think you need more work, Sergeant Brown. It looks to me like you still have a *lot* more soccer to learn."

"Then I guess I'll be sticking around for a long time."

I smiled and kicked the ball toward him.

ACKNOWLEDGMENTS

I would like to thank the following people:

Phoebe Yeh for being so patient and such a wonderful editor. I could not have done this without her.

Amanda Glickman at HarperCollins for keeping everything running smoothly.

Roberta Fox, attorney, who helped me better understand legal issues.

Mr. Tom Turnbull for not only being a wonderful soccer teacher but a life teacher.

Mr. Glen Kurz, a great English teacher and amazing wrestling coach.

Mr. John Cheddar and Mr. Don McDonald for helping instill discipline and being fantastic wrestling coaches.

My mom for believing in me.

My dad and brother for being so supportive.

Last and most important, I want to thank Walter Dean Myers for giving me this life-changing opportunity. I will always be grateful.

—R.W.

Critically acclaimed author **WALTER DEAN MYERS** has garnered much respect and admiration for his fiction, nonfiction, and poetry for young people. Winner of the first Michael L. Printz Award, five Coretta Scott King Awards, two Newbery Honors, and the first-ever Coretta Scott King–Virginia Hamilton Award for Lifetime Achievement, he is considered one of the preeminent writers for children. He lives in Jersey City, New Jersey, with his family. You can visit him online at www.walterdeanmyers.net.

When **ROSS WORKMAN** was thirteen, he wrote a fan email to his favorite author. When Walter Dean Myers wrote back and asked him whether he would be interested in writing a book, Ross was amazed—and incredibly excited. Four years later, Ross is seventeen and in eleventh grade at Westfield Senior High School. In addition to writing, Ross plays a sport every season: high school soccer in the fall, high school wrestling in the winter, and club travel soccer in the spring. He lives in Westfield, New Jersey.